THE LAST GOODBYE

MIA KENT

The Last Goodbye

By Mia Kent

Be the first to know about new releases! Sign up for my newsletter here. Your information will never be shared.

❀ Created with Vellum

CHAPTER 1

*L*ydia Showalter gripped the handle of her coffee mug and tried not to stare at the young mother sitting at the table beside her, cooing and making silly faces at her baby, who was in his stroller, kicking his plump little legs as fast as he could in delight. He was adorable, with rosy cheeks, six scraggly teeth, and clear blue eyes that sparkled as he let loose a belly laugh that made Lydia wince, her grip on the mug tightening even further.

Five years had passed, but the pain was ever-present, a nagging, tugging feeling on her soul that sometimes made breathing difficult. She'd thought that distance would help. She'd thought that putting the past behind her would allow her to heal. It hadn't. Now, she was about to come face to face with her decisions—and the idea of seeing his face again, of hearing his voice, was almost more than she could stand.

"Lydia? Hi, sorry I'm late."

Maura Grant, the bride-to-be, slid into the chair opposite Lydia and pushed her Chanel sunglasses over her head. She snapped her fingers at the waitress, then dug a bulging binder out of her designer bag and slapped it down on the table between them, sending paper napkins flying. One landed on the baby's knees, and he let out another giggle that Lydia did her best to tune out as she apologized to the mother and tugged it out of his chubby fingers.

Then she returned her attention to her client, who was huffing with impatience and preparing to snap her fingers again. The waitress, looking heckled, caught her eye and hurried over, then waited a full two minutes, pen poised over her notepad, while Maura wavered between the green tea and the chai latte.

"It's just so hard to get good service these days," Maura hissed as the waitress left to prepare her drink.

Lydia could tell by the sudden stiffness in the woman's shoulders that she had overheard the insult, and she sighed inwardly, making a mental note to leave an extra-large tip in the jar by the counter before she left. As a wedding planner, Lydia was used to demanding, self-centered brides who truly believed that the sun rose and set only for them, but Maura Grant, daughter of Milton Grant, a tech industry bigwig who was sparing no expense for his only child's big day, definitely took the cake.

Maura was a brat, plain and simple. She'd grown up with a silver—no, scratch that, a *golden*—spoon in her mouth, and as such, she expected everyone, Lydia included, to acquiesce to her every whim and desire, however fanciful or over the top, no matter how much extra work it required. This wedding had tried Lydia's patience—and her professionalism—to its absolute limits, although, to be fair, she had learned a few interesting things along the way.

Like how to apply for a fireworks permit, for one. And that an elephant could not, no matter the circumstances, be transported via ferry to an island off the coast of Maine, regardless of how much the bride wanted to ride into her reception on one... and despite how much she screamed at Lydia for being unable to make it happen.

But finally, *finally*, after an excruciatingly long twelve months, the wedding day was almost upon them. In less than seven days, Lydia would never have to see Maura Grant's face again.

And she wouldn't have to see Luke's, either.

Lydia took a deep breath, reminding herself once more that she needed to focus on the task at hand, and not on the fact that she would be confronted with him again for the first time in five years.

Her ex-husband.

She'd always hated that word, and never believed it would apply to Luke, the boy she had loved since she was a teenager. But they'd been unable to overcome their heartache, and ultimately, that had led to their undoing.

Correction: *she'd* been unable to overcome their heartache. Luke had begged her to stay.

"Are you even, like, paying attention?" Maura's gaze was sharp on Lydia's face, and when Lydia blinked, dragging herself back into the present moment, it was to see her client flicking her long blonde hair over her shoulders and scowling in annoyance.

"Sorry," Lydia said, sliding her notebook out of her purse and setting it on the table. "I was just trying to remember if you said you were expecting a hundred and five guests, or a hundred and seven."

"That's exactly what I wanted to talk to you about."

Maura crossed one long leg over the other and examined her perfectly manicured fingernails as her massive engagement ring caught the coffee shop's overhead lighting and sparkled almost obscenely. That rock had surely cost more than Lydia made in a year—heck, it probably cost more than she made in a *decade*. Lydia would be terrified to wear that thing around town, but she'd be even more terrified to wear it around the house. What if it slipped off in the sink while Maura was washing the dishes?

Then she snorted to herself. The haughty twenty-something sitting across from her had probably never lifted a finger to do a chore in her life.

"—won't be a problem, right? It's only an extra hundred people, give or take."

Lydia straightened in her chair as she realized that, once again, her thoughts had drifted away. No matter how much she had come to dislike Maura over the past year, she was still Lydia's client, which meant she deserved her undivided attention. Right now, though, Lydia was having a hard time giving it to her—and for good reason. Ever since Maura had changed the location of her wedding and reception to Dolphin Bay, Lydia had been walking around in a fog, trying to figure out how she could avoid attending it.

She could tell Maura she broke her leg. She could *actually* break her leg. She could throw herself off the ferry on the way to the island, swim back to shore, and then disappear forever. Maybe even change her name.

Anything, *anything*, to avoid having to look into his eyes again.

"So that's okay, right?"

Maura was picking at an imaginary speck of dirt beneath her fingernail, one sculpted eyebrow arched as she smiled sweetly at Lydia, who was scrambling to recall anything Maura had said over the past two minutes.

"Sure, whatever you want. You *are* the bride, after all." Lydia's smile was tight as she said those last words, which she'd come to understand were important for Maura to hear at least thirty-seven times a week. "So as I was saying, we'll need to have the final guest count by tomorrow morning so we can provide those details to the caterer, and then tomorrow afternoon I'm going to swing by the florist with those crystal vases you ordered. Your flower shipment is being flown in on Thursday evening, which will give him enough time to..."

She trailed off as she realized that Maura was no longer listening; instead, she was gazing at an elderly couple who had just walked into the coffee shop, her arm tucked inside his, their heads bent together as they laughed over some private joke. "Do you think Jared and I will ever be like them?" she asked, twisting her engagement ring absentmindedly around on her finger. "Do you think we'll, like, make it?"

Maura tore her eyes away from the couple and gave Lydia a wry smile. "Not a single person in my family is married to their first spouse. My mom is with Grant, and my dad—well, let's see. After my mom—or I should say *during* my mom—there was Olivia." She began ticking names off on her fingers. "Then Lana, Pamela, and now Darcy." She rolled her eyes. "Who, by the way, is three years younger than me. She thinks it's hilarious that she's my stepmom. I think it's gross."

Maura shuddered, then her eyes drifted to Lydia's bare ring finger, which she covered self-consciously. It had become a point of contention in her own mind that she spent her days planning lavish weddings for brides when her own marriage had been a failure. Lydia winced, preparing herself for the question that would surely follow, but

7

Maura, ever the narcissist, merely shrugged and flipped open her binder.

Lydia watched her for a moment, her eyes trailing over the photos of wedding gowns and flower bouquets and centerpieces that she and Maura had painstakingly been collecting over the past year. Soon, the wedding would be over, and then what? Real life for the newlywed couple would begin.

And sometimes, real life could be brutal.

"I don't know," she said softly, her memories drifting back to her own special day, and the look of absolute love on Luke's face as her father walked her down the aisle. He had been so handsome, and so young. They had been so innocent, so naïve, with no inkling of the heartaches that would soon come their way. They had taken it for granted that their life would be perfect, that their love for each other would overcome all else.

"Hmm?" Maura said in a distracted voice without glancing up from the binder. "You don't know what?"

"I don't know if you'll make it."

At this, Maura's head whipped up. "Why would you say a thing like that? I'm getting married in, like, less than a *week*. Aren't you supposed to be supporting me? I'm pretty sure Daddy's paying you good money for that."

Lydia's cheeks flared, but she crossed her arms over her chest, feeling mildly defiant. "I'm only answering the question you asked me. You and your husband might make it, and you might not. That's going to depend on both of you." She pushed aside the memory of Luke's smiling face as they shared their first dance. They had swayed in each other's arms beneath the soft lights, and even though the ballroom had been filled with people, they only had eyes for each other.

When Lydia spoke next, she softened her voice; after all, it wasn't Maura's fault that her world had fallen apart. "Does he support you? Do you support him? Are you each other's biggest cheerleaders? When life gets hard—and it will—will you turn to each other, or will you turn away? Planning a wedding is fun, but it's just a single day, one of thousands you're going to have together. In all the stress and excitement, everyone forgets that they're not really planning a wedding—they're planning a marriage."

She leaned across the table and rested her hand on Maura's. "The day is going to come when his hair is gray and he has a little trouble getting out of bed in the morning. And when that happens, if he's still your favorite person in the world, the one you couldn't imagine living without... then yes, you'll make it."

Maura was silent for several long moments after that. Her eyes flicked once more to the elderly couple, who were now holding hands across the table, and something indecipherable flashed across her face—regret, maybe? Or maybe those were Lydia's own feelings being reflected back at her.

The baby at the table next to them let out a screech, and Maura gave a start. She tossed her long hair over her shoulders once more, then returned her attention to the binder, pulling it toward herself and flicking to the page that showcased the elegant gold chivari chairs she'd chosen. "So we'll be able to order another hundred of these and have them delivered to the reception in time. Maybe a hundred and twenty to be on the safe side, in case we decide to add a few more couples to the list."

Lydia squinted at her client, scratching her chin with the eraser end of her pencil, certain she had misheard. "When you say a hundred and twenty, you mean five more than the original order of a hundred and fifteen?" She flipped through her notes to double-check the guest list Maura and Jared had submitted to her several months ago. "I suppose we can make that work. I'll have to call the—"

"No." Maura was shaking her head in annoyance. "An *extra* hundred and twenty. For a total of two hundred and thirty-five." She resumed examining her manicure.

"Sorry." Lydia stared at her blankly. "I'm not sure I'm following what you're saying here. Why would you need two hundred and thirty-five chairs for a little over a hundred guests? We're going to be using the same chairs at the reception as we are at the ceremony—the venue staff is going to move them during the cocktail hour."

Maura heaved a long-suffering sigh. "Like, I don't get why you're not understanding this. Jared and I need the extra chairs to accommodate the extra guests we invited last night. Daddy and I talked about it, and he gave me the okay to extend invitations to our B-list. He told me to tell you not to worry about the money—you'll have everything you need." She sat back in her chair, satisfied, while Lydia gaped at her in horror, frantically trying to work out where she had missed this little tidbit of information.

"You—you can't add over a hundred guests a week before the wedding," she spluttered, her cheeks going red. "That means double the work for the caterer, the florist, the bakery, the rental company who's setting up the tables and chairs…"

Lydia ticked off the long list of vendors on her fingers as she spoke, shaking her head in disbelief. "Everything's been ordered and signed off on—there's no way to do that in such a short period of time. I can *maybe* buy you an extra ten, fifteen guests at the most. The vendors will never agree to anything different."

"Well," Maura said, gathering her binder and purse in her arms and standing from the table, leaving her tea untouched, "that's for you to figure out, isn't it? Gotta run—I'm meeting Daddy for lunch, and don't worry, I'll be sure to tell him you've got this handled."

She gave Lydia a wink that sent a wave of fury washing over her. "After all, I'm pretty sure your reputation in this town depends on it."

CHAPTER 2

*D*aphne Hall tied her apron around her waist as she stepped inside Sal's Diner and glanced around, trying to gauge the size of the morning crowd. Summertime on the island was still in full swing, which meant that most days started off with a line of hungry customers waiting for tables and the scent of bacon grease wafting through the air. She called a greeting to several of the harried-looking waitresses who were hurrying past, balancing trays of coffee, orange juice, pancakes, and eggs as they wove through the bustling restaurant.

"Hey, doll," Betty, the hostess, called out, smiling as Daphne stopped at her station to say good morning. "I sure am glad to see you—the new gals are having a hard time keeping up with the crowd today.

Jenny's already dropped an omelet and a stack of waffles on the carpet—you shoulda seen the steam coming out of Sal's ears when he heard the commotion and saw the mess." She sighed. "I don't mind the tips in the summer, but I'll tell ya—I can't wait for September."

"I hear you," Daphne said, grabbing a pad of paper and stuffing a handful of pencils into the pocket of her apron. "Fall will be here before we know it, and when that happens, we can all finally sit down and take a breather."

"Yeah," Betty said with a chuckle. "And count down the days until Sal and the missus take their annual vacation. It's more relaxing than my own." She winked at Daphne, who laughed appreciatively, though her insides were squirming with guilt. The truth was, she was going to be gone before the summer tourist rush ended.

And she'd finally be giving Sal the news today.

He needed to be the first to know that his most experienced waitress was leaving—that, in fact, she already had one foot out the door. In a town as small as Dolphin Bay, Daphne couldn't believe that her secret hadn't slipped out yet, but she had only confided in a handful of people, and they had promised they wouldn't share the news with anyone until the time was right.

And finally, *finally*, that time was now. For the past couple of months, in between her shifts at the diner, Daphne had been holed up in the small shop on the island's main drag that would soon transform into the real-life version of what, until now, had only been a dream.

A bakery of her own.

She could hardly dare to believe it was actually happening, but the contracts were signed, the recipes finalized, the supplies purchased… and in two short weeks, the "Grand Opening" sign would be hung.

As that image played across her mind, Daphne wove through the diner's crowded interior toward the kitchen, where she knew she would find Sal, red-faced and sweating, barking orders to the staff as the smell of grease stained the air and the clatter and bang of pots and pans rose to near-deafening levels. The diner's owner was intimidating on a good day, and even though Daphne had been putting up with his antics since the tender age of sixteen, she had been dreading this moment for weeks.

Drawing in a deep breath, she pushed open the swinging door and stepped inside the kitchen, her eyes skating over the grill cooks and busboys until she found the man she was looking for. Sal was standing over the massive griddle, his hands flying as he expertly flipped omelets, stacked pancakes, and poured batter onto the smoking surface. His face was beet-red and his balding head was shining with sweat, which he was sopping up with a bundle of paper towels plastered to his scalp.

Even though her boss looked to be on the verge of a perpetual heart attack, Daphne knew that he lived for the diner, which he had opened as a boy barely out of high school with a small inheritance he had received from his grandfather. He had single-handedly built his namesake diner into the most popular eatery on the island, which Daphne knew was something to be celebrated. She only hoped she would find the same success in her own business venture someday.

"Sal?" Daphne reached out a hesitant finger and tapped him on the shoulder as a busboy hurried past carrying a towering stack of dishes that looked ready to collapse. "Could I have a word?"

"Give me a minute," he barked, not even bothering to turn around. He flipped two waffles onto a plate, added a heaping portion of scrambled eggs, then slid the dish down the line so it could receive its garnishes.

Then he wiped his hands on the grease-stained apron he wore low around his waist and turned, his bushy gray eyebrows rising when he saw Daphne hovering uncertainly behind him. "Shouldn't you be out front taking orders or delivering drinks? I don't have time for my waitresses to be standing around chitchatting."

He swept his arm around the kitchen as if the rest of the wait staff were standing there too. Daphne bit back a sarcastic comment, reminding herself that in fourteen short days, she would be rid of this place—and this insufferable man—for good.

"My shift doesn't start for half an hour," she said in as good-natured a voice as she could muster. "I was hoping I could talk to you for a few minutes." She glanced around the bustling kitchen and noticed a couple of line cooks watching the interaction with interest. The last thing she wanted right now was an audience, so she added, "Alone."

Sal peered at her for a few moments, his eyes scanning her face, and then he shrugged, grabbed a nearby dishtowel, and wiped his hands on it before slinging it over his shoulder. He swung around and began walking away from her, his large frame cutting a path through the kitchen staff, who parted on instinct to let him through. Daphne, taking this as her cue to follow him, hurried to catch up, trailing after him as he made his way to his cramped office.

Daphne had only been inside the small space a handful of times, and today, it was as cluttered as ever—with stacks of papers on every surface, an overflowing trash can, and a desk and computer chair that had seen better days. Sal lowered himself into the chair with a groan, gave his sweat-beaded brow one last dab with the paper towels, then wadded them up and tossed them toward the trash can, missing by several feet.

He shrugged, then leaned back and gestured for Daphne to take the seat across from him. "How can I help you, sweetheart?"

Daphne cringed at the nickname, which she hated with a passion. Sal was about as old-school as they came, a man who truly believed that men ruled the roost and women lived to serve them. How he had been married for four decades was beyond Daphne's comprehension, although she had met his wife on several occasions and had a feeling she knew who really wore the pants in that relationship.

Her eyes roamed around the claustrophobic room as she stalled for time, trying once again to figure out how best to break the news to Sal that she was leaving. From an outsider's perspective, her nerves were probably laughable—after all, she was just quitting a job, something that thousands of people around the world did every day. But for Daphne, working at Sal's was part of her identity, part of the very fabric of her life. No matter how much she was ready to leave, no matter how much she *needed* to leave, for her own sake, nothing about this had seemed real until this very moment.

Sal cleared his throat, looking impatient, and Daphne forced herself to meet his gaze. "I'm leaving, Sal. Two weeks from tomorrow will be my last day."

She sat back in the chair and exhaled softly, feeling an enormous weight being lifted off her shoulders, though she couldn't truly relax until she had finished convincing Sal that she was really leaving for good—because she already knew there was no way he was letting her go without a fight. She gave him an expectant look, waiting for him to process the news.

He opened his mouth to say something, then changed his mind and shrugged instead. "Okay. Make sure you leave your apron with Betty before you go. We'll have it cleaned for the next girl." Then he heaved himself up from the desk, bracing both hands against the wood, and lumbered out of the room, not even bothering to look back.

Daphne watched the door swing closed in stunned silence, her mind numb with disbelief.

Twenty-seven years. She had spent twenty-seven *years* at this place, and that hadn't even earned her a proper goodbye. Or, heaven forbid, a thank you. Sal had just solidified what she had always feared to be true: she was expendable, and always had been.

Well, not anymore.

The wooden chair made a sharp scraping sound against the office's worn linoleum floor as Daphne stood quietly, untied her apron, and tossed it onto Sal's desk.

Thirty seconds later, she was marching out the diner's front door, never to look back.

"Sir, can I help you with anything?"

Luke Showalter's head shot up and he blinked at the older woman standing beside him, smiling warmly and gesturing to the refrigerated case of flowers in front of him. He felt a rush of embarrassment as he realized he'd been standing there for several minutes, staring blankly at the bouquets of flowers without even seeing them.

"Might I suggest some of these?" The florist wiped her hands on her dirt-stained apron and closed the distance between them, and Luke could smell the subtle scent of her perfume as she bent over and gently lifted a bouquet of dusky purple roses wreathed in baby's breath from the case. "They're quite rare; only a handful of growers in all of Maine attempt them."

When Luke automatically winced and shook his head at the sight of the roses—they had been Lydia's favorite, his gift to her on all sorts of happy occasions—the woman regarded him with a slight frown. "I'm sorry, I shouldn't have assumed..." She gestured toward a bundle of gladiolas instead. "If you're looking to deliver flowers to a funeral home or cemetery, then—"

"No." Luke shook his head again, this time more fervently, and sighed as he ran a hand through his hair. This little excursion was turning out to be much more complicated than he had ever imagined. Then again, he hadn't given flowers to a woman in five years... well, more than that, if he wanted to get technical about it. His marriage had been troubled for a long time before its ultimate demise, and if he was being honest with himself, he couldn't remember the last time he had surprised Lydia with something to put a smile on her face.

Still feeling the florist's gaze on him, Luke glanced around the small shop, his eyes landing on a bouquet of cheerful-looking sunflowers that definitely didn't say *I love you*. More like, *I think you're swell*.

Perfect. And perfectly ridiculous.

"I'll take those," he said, then, decision made, he followed the woman to the front counter, watching as she wrapped the flowers in green tissue paper and added an intricate bow at the bottom. As if sensing his discomfort, she didn't attempt to make any small talk with him, merely accepting his credit card with a nod and then passing him the flowers with a smile before waving him out the door.

Luke exhaled an enormous breath he hadn't realized he'd been holding as he stepped onto the sidewalk, the bouquet tucked under his arm. It was another beautiful day on the island, but the brilliant sun and the crystalline sky couldn't brighten the funk he'd felt himself slipping into ever since he'd answered the phone and heard her voice. Two months had passed since then, the blink of an eye when time was steadily marching toward the day he'd been dreading for the past five years, when she packed her bags and left him without warning.

How was he supposed to face her again?

Her call was a pity call—that much he knew. She'd wanted to warn him that she'd be in town for a wedding she was planning, and didn't want to catch him off guard when they likely ran into each other right in the middle of Main Street. He was grateful for that, at least. But in truth, he didn't know which was worse: a chance meeting with the woman who had broken him, or, as was the case now, an excruciating countdown to the day she would arrive. The last two months had been practically unendurable for him; the only thing helping him maintain his sanity was the woman he was going to see now.

He smiled as he thought of Daphne, then turned and began making his way down the sidewalk, his fingers tightening around the bouquet of flowers. Over the past couple of months, what had started as a mentoring relationship had quickly progressed to friendship, and now, the possibility of something more was blooming between them. Daphne was a wonderful woman, sweet and good-natured with a heart of gold, and after they spent time together, he often found himself thinking of her as he walked back to his own house—a man could easily get lost in her eyes, which were bluer than a summer sky, and every time he heard her musical laughter, he felt warmed from the inside out.

But so far, their relationship had been strictly platonic—he'd been guiding her through the triumphs and pains of opening a business of her own, and as a small thank you, she'd taken to inviting him over for dinner and a movie several times a week. They'd yet to even hold hands, but the distance between them on the couch was shrinking by the day, and just last night, an exhausted Daphne had fallen asleep during the movie, her head resting on his shoulder as he listened to the soothing sound of her steady breathing. It had been both foreign and exciting—Luke hadn't felt anything for another woman since Lydia; was, in fact, positive that he never would again.

But maybe, just maybe, that was beginning to change.

Nodding to a group of tourists who were window-shopping at a small souvenir store that had been in business on the island since Luke was a child, he skirted around them and approached Daphne's shop. He had to hand it to her—even though she had no prior experience owning a business, she had taken to the job with an ease and professionalism that made it seem as though she'd been doing it all her life. They were way ahead of schedule, and even though the bakery wouldn't be celebrating its grand opening for another two weeks, everything was ready to go—Daphne just needed to fill the bakery's cases with her homemade cakes, pies, cookies, and other treats, and Luke was positive that the island's residents and tourists alike would flock to her.

He spotted her through a gap in the bakery's blinds, standing behind the counter, elbows bent on the surface, long blonde hair falling over her face. She always kept the blinds drawn tightly whenever she was working inside; according to Daphne, it was because she didn't want anyone at Sal's Diner to know she was leaving her waitressing job until the time was right.

But Luke knew better—Daphne was terrified of unveiling her bakery to the island, and everyone she knew. Even though her talent as a baker was undeniable, and she was the kind of woman who easily won over friends and admirers, she suffered from a lack of confidence that had, at times, threatened to derail her. Luke had done his best to guide her through the fears and uncertainties while also assuring her that those feelings were perfectly normal. Heck, he *still* had days when he had difficulty trusting in his own abilities, and he'd owned his contracting business for almost twenty years.

"Hey," he said brightly, opening the bakery's door before slipping inside and quickly closing it behind him.

Daphne gave a start and glanced up from the counter, and he saw that her face was furrowed into a frown. "You won't believe the day I've had," she began, and then, catching sight of the flowers, her expression softened. "What's all this?"

Luke stepped forward to greet her, hesitating for the barest of moments before kissing her lightly on the cheek. "These are for you," he said, pulling back from her and pressing the bouquet into her arms. "Today was a big day—congratulations."

Daphne's eyes searched his face, a question evident in her gaze, but she didn't press him on the kiss. Instead, she raised the bouquet to her nose and inhaled deeply, then laughed as she set them gently on the counter. "It was an even bigger day than you know—as of this morning, I'm no longer employed at Sal's Diner." She pressed a hand to her cheek and shook her head in wonder. "I can't even believe I'm saying those words—I've practically lived at the place since I was a teenager, and I always assumed

I'd be there until I retired. But now, I'm a free woman." She spread her arms wide to indicate the bakery. "If this ship sinks, I'm going down with it."

"The bakery isn't sinking, and neither are you," Luke said as he led Daphne to one of the small bistro tables she'd set up in the shop for those who wanted to enjoy a cup of coffee and a pastry while taking in the views of Dolphin Bay's stunning coastline. "But I don't get it—I thought you were just putting in your notice today. What changed?"

"What changed is that I realized no one cared if I left." Daphne's eyes darkened with anger, but beneath it, Luke could see the hurt in them. "You'd think, after twenty-seven years, the least that miserable man could do was thank me for all the extra things I did for him, the unpaid overtime and the endless shifts I covered and the holidays I volunteered to work when no one else would. I would have even settled for a goodbye."

She was quiet for several long moments, staring down at her hands, and then she laughed quietly. "It always hurts to realize how little you mean to someone."

Luke's mind immediately flashed to Lydia, but he tamped down on the image of her face as quickly as it had popped up. "I understand," he said softly, reaching across the small table to cover Daphne's hand with his own. He waited for her to glance up, and then he grinned at her. "But look on the bright side—now you have two extra weeks to relax before the grand opening. No rude customers to deal with, no bad tips, no aching feet at the end of the day…"

"Oh, yes," Daphne said playfully. "I can't wait to spend the next fourteen days by myself, with nothing to distract me, fretting about all the things that could possibly go wrong. Like—"

Luke cut her off with a shake of his head and a fierce look. "Let's not start that again. In fact, I think we should take the rest of the day off from thinking about the bakery at all. I was wondering…" He hesitated as the idea that had been lingering in the back of his mind for weeks finally made it to the forefront. He had been toying with it, turning it over and over in his head, trying to reconcile his growing feelings for Daphne with his inability to move on from the devastation Lydia had wrought on his life, and on his heart.

He didn't know if he was ready to move on. He didn't know if he ever would be. But he also knew that he had to try.

Daphne was watching him curiously now, her head cocked, her lips parted in confusion. Forcing himself back to the present moment, he allowed the hesitations to roll off his shoulders—for now, at least —and reached for her hand again. "I was wondering if you might let me take you out for dinner. And this time, not as friends."

Visibly caught off guard, Daphne exhaled softly, and then a smile lit up her beautiful face. "I would love that," she said, giving his hand a gentle squeeze. "What time should I be ready?"

As they finalized their plans, Luke did his best to ignore the feeling of wrongness creeping up on him as his eyes lingered on Daphne's, which were lit up with excitement. But a few minutes later, when he walked out of the bakery with a promise to pick her up in a few hours, her face was the one playing across his mind.

He made sure of it.

CHAPTER 3

"*I* can't believe it. It's... beautiful."

Tana felt her eyes welling up with tears as Reed stood beside her, his arm wrapped tightly around her waist, both of them gazing at the first of the Inn at Dolphin Bay's newly renovated guest rooms. Luke and his crew had finished packing up late last night, but Tana had forced herself to wait until morning to see the results of the past few months of hard work, sweat, and—she wasn't ashamed to admit it—plenty of tears on her part. When she'd stepped foot on the island for the first time in more than two decades, she could hardly believe what had happened to the beautiful inn where she and her brother had made so many happy memories.

In that moment, she had grieved its loss. Now, she was witnessing its rebirth.

"It does look stunning," Reed said, releasing Tana to trail his fingers along the walls, now painted a soft gray-blue that mirrored the color of the sea that swelled outside the room's sparkling-clean window. Then he turned to the furniture, a stylish mix of cream-colored, beach-inspired pieces that were artfully weathered, before admiring the seascape painting that hung on the wall over the bed, which was adorned with new bedding and soft pillows. The old, musty carpet had been replaced with gleaming hardwood floors finished in a trendy gray, and a beautiful gas fireplace beckoned warmth and invitation from the corner of the room.

Tana had a major hand in the inn's new look, but now, seeing all of her visions come to life… the feeling was almost overwhelming.

"I'm so proud of you," Reed said, squeezing her hand before pulling her in for a gentle kiss. Then he stepped back, his pale blue eyes searching hers, a soft smile on his lips. "This—all of it—is because of your dedication to the inn, and to your uncle. If you hadn't stepped in, the inn might have been lost forever. He's lucky to have you in his life."

"Stop," Tana said, dabbing her eyes with a tissue

and finding the effort futile as more tears continued to flow. "The inn would never have been what it was without Uncle Henry's love and dedication. I'm just helping to make it shine again—he already put in the work." She sighed happily. "But this renovation has given me a welcome change in my life, a reason to focus on the good"—she squeezed his hand happily —"and remove myself from the bad."

They both knew, of course, that Tana was referring to Derek, her soon-to-be ex-husband and the man who had broken her heart. Even though she had been devastated by the brutal end to a decades-long marriage, that too had a silver lining... and it came in the form of the man standing beside her.

"I love you," she whispered, standing on tiptoe to press a soft kiss to his stubbled cheek. "Thank you for everything you've given me."

"I'm the one who should be thanking you." Reed cupped her chin lightly. "These past few months have been... indescribable."

"Listen to them, Henry. Why don't you say such sweet things to me?" Edie teased, causing both Tana and Reed to swing around in surprise. The older couple was standing shoulder to shoulder in the doorway, Edie's eyes sparkling with mischief, Henry leaning awkwardly on his cane.

"I do say sweet things to you," he shot back, looking uncomfortable. "Don't you remember after dinner last night? I told you that your kitchen was the cleanest one I'd ever been in. I meant it, too."

"Such a charmer." Edie shot him a dubious look, then elbowed him playfully. "Now come on, let's join these two lovebirds. I've been dying to see the inn ever since Henry told me Luke and his crew had finally finished."

She stepped into the room and whistled appreciatively. "Tana, this is stunning. You outdid yourself —it's the perfect blend of comfortable and stylish. The guests are going to love it."

She joined Reed in admiring the new furniture as Tana stepped back to give them space. The thump-thumping of Henry's cane against the wood floors alerted her to his movement, and she turned to find him standing beside her.

"You did good, kid." He rested a hand on her shoulder, and she reached up to give it a soft squeeze. The words were high praise from her great-uncle, a man of few words and fewer emotions—at least on the outside. His relationship with Edie was softening him, though, and when Tana's gaze caught his, she could have sworn she caught sight of a few tears shining in the old man's green eyes before he turned and thumped away.

She was about to join Reed and his mother, who were now standing at the window, admiring the ocean view, when she felt her cell phone buzzing in her pocket. She slipped it out and glanced at the caller ID, grinning as she saw her daughter Emery's name. Excusing herself, she stepped into the hallway and accepted the call.

"Emery, honey, it's so nice to hear from you. How are you?"

Tana and her daughter had always been close, and even though they spoke on the phone often, the physical distance between them made her heart ache. Emery was now a grown woman studying fashion design in New York City, but to Tana, she would always be the little girl with the raven hair glistening in the sunshine as she blew bubbles and twirled around the backyard, arms spread wide, tiny face tipped up to the sky.

"Hey, Mom, how's it going?"

Emery's voice was clear and upbeat, which made Tana's heart soar with happiness. Even though their daughter was grown, Tana and Derek's divorce had been difficult on their only child; what had seemed like a fairy-tale romance all throughout her childhood had imploded without warning, leaving her with a lot of bitterness toward her father. Tana had been helping Emery work through her anger toward Derek over the past couple of months, because as much as she resented her husband for what he had done, she didn't want her daughter to suffer from a strained relationship, especially since father and daughter had always shared a close bond.

Slowly, cautiously, Emery had begun letting him back into her life, and while Tana knew that they were speaking on the phone periodically, she wasn't privy to the details—nor did she want to be. She wasn't keen on maintaining any kind of relationship with Derek beyond one of basic civility when discussing matters related to their child, or the details of their divorce. The six-month waiting period before that would officially happen was ticking by steadily; helped along, of course, by Tana throwing everything she had into the inn and her new life in Dolphin Bay. These days, the memories of her life in California were starting to dim, Derek's betrayal a lingering pain in the pit of her stomach that was lessening each week.

With that in mind, Tana trailed her fingers along the hallway's newly painted walls and said to her daughter, "I'm good. Great, actually. The inn is about to celebrate its grand reopening—all the renovations are finally finished, and the end result is simply stunning."

"That's wonderful, Mom, I can't wait to see it. And on that note, I know how hard you've been working these past couple of months, so I sent you a little gift—it was delivered to the inn just a few minutes ago."

"Really?" Tana glanced at her watch; the mail wasn't due to arrive until late afternoon, and she hadn't noticed a package being delivered. She bounded down the steps and hurried through the foyer, eager to see what her daughter might have sent—she knew Emery was working on creating a line of women's accessories for a school project, and the pictures she'd sent last week of the stunning silk scarves she had designed made Tana's entire body ache with pride. She'd had her eye on one with a swirling teal and gray pattern that would pair perfectly with a dress she and Daphne had picked out while on a shopping trip to the mainland a few weeks ago.

A quick glance at the front door revealed no package waiting outside, so Tana stepped out onto the inn's beautiful wraparound porch—freshly painted and now accessorized with brand-new outdoor gliders and Adirondack chairs with comfortable cushions. Tana had to admit, though, that she missed the battered wicker chair that overlooked the sea and had quickly become her safe place when she first arrived on the island, more than a little battered herself.

But the porch, too, was empty—as was the inn's cobblestone walkway and gravel driveway. "Sorry, honey," Tana said, putting the phone back to her ear with a shrug. "I don't think it's arrived yet—"

And then she let out an involuntary gasp when her daughter rounded the corner of the inn and made a beeline for her, arms outstretched, face lit up with an ear-to-ear grin. They threw their arms around each other, Tana holding her daughter as tightly as she could, breathing in the familiar lavender scent of her shampoo before pulling back to look at her.

"What are you doing here?" she said, tugging Emery up the porch steps and leading her to a pair of comfortable rocking chairs on the side of the inn that overlooked the island's stunning red-and-white lighthouse. "I thought you had to stay in New York for the entire summer. What about your classes?"

"Done for the semester." Emery grinned at her mother. "I have a three-week break before fall classes begin, and I wanted to surprise you—and see the inn, of course." She glanced around the porch, then gazed out over the beautiful sweeping views of the harbor and the gently rolling ocean beyond. "This place is amazing—your descriptions haven't done it justice. I'm dying to see the inside. And meet Uncle Henry, of course. He sounds like quite a character."

"That's putting it mildly." Tana laughed and reached over to grip her daughter's hand. "Thank you so much for coming here—what a wonderful surprise."

"Yeah, well, I thought it would be good for you. And me, too." Emery's face tightened, and Tana automatically winced, knowing her daughter was reflecting on the difficult events of the past few months.

"How are you doing?" she asked softly, settling back in her chair and joining Emery in gazing out at the sun-dappled surface of the water. "You know, with… everything."

The late-morning sunshine was highlighting the strands of amber in Emery's dark hair as she ran a frustrated hand through it and shook her head. "I'm angry. But mostly hurt, I think. When he left you, he left me too."

Tana shook her head fiercely. "No, don't—"

"Mom, I have to tell you something," Emery interrupted, inhaling deeply and letting out a long sigh. She dropped her hands into her lap and began twisting her fingers together nervously, then balled her hands into fists. "I've been trying to figure out the best time to do it, but over the phone seemed like a bad idea. But I also don't want to ruin our time here together, and... Oh, I don't know." She grabbed her purse and rummaged through it angrily, then withdrew a tissue and dabbed at her eyes.

By now, Tana was holding her breath, her mind whirling as she tried to guess just what type of awful news her daughter was trying to break to her. Was she sick? Hurt? Was she dropping out of school? Moving across the world? Eloping with a man she only met a week ago? Her chest tightened with fear, and she leaned forward in her chair and gripped her daughter's wrist, forcing her to meet her gaze. "Tell me. Please."

Emery blinked hard a few times, then wiped at her eyes roughly with the tissue one last time before beginning to methodically shred it into long strips that drifted to the porch's wooden floor-boards. "It's Dad," she finally said. "He's... *engaged*." She said the last word as though it were dirty, her lips pressed together so hard they were turning white. "To *her*," she added, as if Tana needed the clarification.

Tana's free hand automatically clenched the armrest of her chair as the unfairness of it all settled over her like a shroud.

Derek was marrying his mistress. They hadn't even signed the divorce papers yet, and he was already planning to spend his life with the same woman who had helped to ruin hers.

No. Not ruined.

Tana shook her head, internally correcting herself. With the same woman who had *changed* hers. And in many ways, for the better. That didn't stop the sharp stab of pain that ran through her at the thought of Derek at the altar with someone else, though, saying the same words he'd pledged to Tana what seemed like the blink of an eye ago, when their whole lives were stretched before them, shimmering with possibilities.

"Mom?" Emery's cheeks were stained with tears now as she stood and approached Tana, kneeling down and wrapping her in a long hug. "Are you okay?" she asked, her voice muffled against Tana's shoulder. "I'm so sorry I had to be the one to tell you —I just didn't want you to find out from someone else. Or, God forbid, from one of those awful tabloid magazines."

She pulled back from Tana and gave a full-body shudder. "They think that… that *woman* is someone to be celebrated because she can stand in front of a camera and look pretty. But I don't even need to meet her to know that she isn't one-*twentieth* of the person you are. She should be ashamed of herself. Her and Daddy both. I'm not going to the wedding, and I hope he doesn't expect me to. I would never do that to you."

Emery crossed her arms over her chest and pouted her lips, looking for all the world like the eleven-year-old girl who was demanding that Tana let her go to the mall alone with her friends. Tana stifled an automatic smile behind her hands at the memory of those turbulent pre-teen years, simultaneously glad those days were over and mourning them with her whole heart. Such was the mystery of being a parent, she supposed.

"Hey, Tana, is everything—oh. I'm so sorry, I didn't mean to interrupt." Reed stepped out onto the front porch and immediately turned to head back into the house, but Tana stopped him with a wave and a smile.

"Please, stay. There's someone here I'd like you to meet."

Tana stood to greet Reed with a hug and a kiss on the cheek, noticing, out of the corner of her eye, that Emery's eyebrows were raised. She had told her daughter a few details about Reed, not wanting to keep their relationship a secret, but in truth, she had downplayed how serious they were becoming. Emery had been dealing with enough surprising news over the past few months, and even though Tana was confident that her daughter would be happy for her—especially in light of Derek's engagement—she didn't want to turn her world even more upside down than it already was. Now that Emery was in Dolphin Bay, however, there would be no hiding the fact that she and Reed were in love.

"Reed Dawes," Tana said, tugging him gently over to where Emery was sitting, "I'd like you to meet my daughter, Emery Martin. She's here in town for a few weeks—she planned a wonderful surprise visit for me."

"Emery, I'm so glad to meet you." Reed stepped forward to shake her hand, then tucked his arm securely around Tana's waist. "I've heard so much about you. How's life in New York City? I've never been there myself."

"It's indescribable," Emery said, her face lighting up for the first time since she had arrived.

Tana was grateful to move the conversation away from Derek—she knew she would need time to process the news of his sudden engagement later, alone, when she could work through her feelings on the matter. Right now, she wanted to push all the negativity out of her head and focus on the present —and the two people standing in front of her, already laughing and chatting and getting along like old friends as Emery regaled Reed with stories of trying to make her way in the big city.

"Well we don't have any of the Michelin-starred restaurants or Broadway shows here in Dolphin Bay," Reed was saying, "but I can't say I'm too upset about that—since moving here, I've discovered how much I love the slower pace, not to mention how friendly everyone is here. And we have the beach, of course."

"That's what I need right now." Emery plopped back into her chair and kicked her feet up on the porch railing, gesturing with one hand toward the ocean sparkling below them. "Rest, relaxation, and a way to forget about all the stuff that's been happening with my dad…" Her voice trailed off as she stared out over the water, and Tana saw Reed slide a quick, questioning glance her way that she pretended not to notice.

Instead, she clapped her hands together, deciding that a change of subject was in order. "Why don't we go inside and I'll whip up some of my famous home-made lemonade. And," she said in a teasing voice, tugging Emery to her feet and linking her arm through her daughter's, "we'll go find Uncle Henry and break the news that he has yet another Martin woman to contend with at his inn. I can't wait to see his face when he finds out."

CHAPTER 4

*L*ydia let the phone fall out of her hand and land on the couch beside her with a soft *thump*. She had done it. She had actually done it. Against all odds, she had managed to convince each and every vendor for Maura and Jared's wedding to work double time over the next couple of days to accommodate the extra hundred guests that had been added at the last minute.

And she felt awful about it. At least Maura's father was willing to shell out enough cash to pay the vendors handsomely for their efforts, but that did little to quell Lydia's sense of guilt—and the rising belief that she was losing control of her client. The icing on the cake of the awful past few days was when Maura decided that the custom-made, one-of-a-kind designer gown she had flown in from an exclusive boutique in Paris didn't have enough pearls on it—so cue the frantic effort, on Lydia's part, to not only track down a seamstress willing to put in the work on such short notice, but to find a jeweler who could deliver a shipment of loose pearls in under twenty-four hours.

To top it all off, Jared, the husband-to-be, had been away on a business trip for the past few weeks, leaving Lydia to deal with an increasingly unhinged Maura all on her own. Even the bride's own mother had opted to book a last-minute mini-trip to the Bahamas to escape the circus this wedding was becoming, with promises to return the night before the big event—though Lydia had her doubts, given the woman's bulging suitcase.

And if Lydia thought things couldn't get any worse, she was wrong. Because only a few hours ago, she'd heard from a friend who'd been vacationing on Dolphin Bay with her husband and kids. Apparently, the family had gone to enjoy the boardwalk in the evening and had run into Luke. Hand-in-hand with another woman.

The image that brought up in Lydia's mind was enough to make her nauseous, which was followed in short order by deep feelings of shame. What did she expect, that he would stay single forever? The man was a catch, and everyone, Lydia included, knew it. The thought of running into Luke in the lead-up to the wedding had been bad enough; now she had to worry about seeing him in the arms of another woman?

He had been her golden boy. Could she really bear to think that someday—possibly someday soon —he would become that to someone else?

No, she couldn't. She'd kept tabs on Luke over the years—from a distance, of course. She knew that he, too, had been practically destroyed by the divorce, and had coped with losing her by throwing himself headlong into his work. That had always been vaguely... satisfying... to Lydia, which, of course, brought up more feelings of self-loathing. She hadn't wanted him to suffer. But, if she was being completely truthful with herself, she knew that she also didn't want him to be happy.

Maybe that made her a monster.

Maybe that made her a woman who had never —and could never—let go of the dreams they'd once shared, before they lay shattered at their feet. She'd had to leave him behind; she had no other choice.

In their shared grief, they were destroying each

other. She had to escape, for his sake as well as her own.

"Knock *knock!*" a familiar voice sing-songed from the hallway outside her door, and Lydia felt her shoulders tense. After a quick internal debate over whether she should pretend to be out running an errand—or, better yet, on that plane to Hawaii she'd been dreaming about for months now—she heaved a sigh, rose from the couch, and padded over to the door.

"Took you long enough," her mother said, barging through the door the moment Lydia tugged it open. Her arms were weighed down with shopping bags, which she dropped on the floor before pulling Lydia to her in a bone-crushing hug. Lydia winced and tried to get away—she loved her mother, she did, but sometimes the woman could be a bit...

Overbearing? Suffocating? More stubborn than a herd of cranky old donkeys?

Lydia, as the only child, was lucky enough to always bear the brunt of her attention. And she knew that right now, the evening before she left for Dolphin Bay, her mother's singular focus would be on her favorite topic of discussion.

"So tomorrow's the big day, isn't it?" she asked, as though she hadn't been counting down the days to

Lydia's return to Dolphin Bay ever since she'd let slip where Maura and Jared's wedding would be. "Are you excited?"

"Things have been hectic for days, so right now, I'm just hoping to relax for a little before the rest of the crazy hits the fan tomorrow," Lydia said, intentionally sidestepping the question. She yawned widely and stretched her arms over her head with a long, loud groan, hoping her mother would take the hint.

She did not. Instead, she began unpacking the shopping bags, unfolding item after item of clothing and spreading them out on Lydia's living room floor. "What's all this?" Lydia asked, eyeing the row of dresses and blouses with suspicion. They were all in her size, but the loud prints and daring patterns were the opposite of the subtle style she embraced as her own.

"Just a few things to brighten up your wardrobe a bit." Her mother looked her up and down with a critical eye as Lydia tugged self-consciously at the oversized T-shirt she had donned the moment she walked in the door after a long day of Maura-related ridiculousness. "You want to knock him off his socks tomorrow, don't you?"

Ah, here it was. Lydia glanced at the clock.

Sooner than expected, too. Usually Wilma Peterson made it a full five minutes in her daughter's presence before she brought up the one and only subject Lydia always begged her not to. The woman was like an out-of-control train, though, barreling into the station with no hope of avoiding the inevitable crash.

Lydia sighed, long and loud. "Trust me, I'm not going to be knocking anyone's socks off, nor will I be trying to. I'll be spending most of the time running around like a chicken with my head cut off, and the rest of it trying to keep the bride tethered to this planet." She massaged her forehead with her fingertips, suddenly feeling exhausted, and very, very overwhelmed. "Mom, please. I can't do this right now. I'm begging you to let it drop."

Wilma hesitated for a moment, casting her eyes down to the clothes laid out beneath her before raising her head and meeting her daughter's gaze steadily. "I'm sorry, Lydia. I can't do that." She crossed the room to the couch, then dropped onto the cushion beside her daughter uninvited and took her hand.

"This is a chance for you to make things right. This is a chance for the two of you to make your way back to each other. Lydia, open your eyes and look at what's right in front of you. A wedding that you're planning being relocated at the last minute to Dolphin Bay? That island is barely a blip on the map, and somehow, you're ending up there again. Don't tell me that's not fate."

Her mother was staring at her with such conviction, such *hope*, that tears of regret and sadness immediately sprang to Lydia's eyes. "It's not fate, it's bad luck," she said, turning away from her mother and wiping her eyes with the back of her hand. "If I hadn't already signed a contract with Maura and Jared, I would have bowed out of the wedding. The thought of going back to Dolphin Bay… it's killing me. If I never stepped foot on that island again, it would be too soon."

Her mother shook her head, looking undeterred. "But you and Luke—"

"There *is* no me and Luke." Lydia was on her feet, her face flushed with anger. "There hasn't been for five years—and a long time before that. Everything we went through, the years of heartache, it ruined us. We were never able to recover. Why now, when I'm finally starting to pick up the pieces of my life and move on, would you want me to see him again? Why split open old wounds?"

Wilma was quiet for a long time after that, the

lines in her face seeming to deepen with sadness. "Lydia," she finally said, "you're my daughter and I love you, so I'm going to tell you a hard truth. I've been watching this mess from the sidelines for years, and I might just be the only one in a position to see things clearly. You—and by all accounts, Luke too— are never going to move on, not really. The two of you belong together—you have since you were fourteen years old—and until you accept that, and try to mend the broken pieces of your relationship, I don't think you'll ever be happy. Not in here." She pressed a hand to her chest, over her heart. "Life is going to throw you all kinds of heartaches—you already know that. Don't add losing your soulmate to the mix."

She got to her feet heavily, gathering up the empty shopping bags and heading for the door. "I'm going to leave you alone now, because I know you don't want me here. But please, think about what I said. And for the sake of all that is good and holy in this world," she added, one hand on the doorknob as she turned back to meet her daughter's gaze, "when you get to that island, go and pay that man a visit. You're still in love with each other, and no amount of pretending otherwise is going to change that."

DAPHNE HUMMED to herself as she stared at the plain tiered cake in front of her with a critical eye. Now that she was no longer waitressing at Sal's Diner— only stopping in one last time to collect her final paycheck from a teary-eyed Betty, glad that at least one person would miss her—she had more time on her hands to practice the next skill she was hoping to master in preparation for her bakery's grand opening: cake decorating. It was an art unto itself, and even though Daphne prided herself on being able to master even the most complicated pastry recipe, it turned out that piping a straight line of icing was a talent that completely escaped her.

Despite having to start from scratch on no fewer than five practice cakes, she'd had a smile on her face the entire day, thanks to another wonderful date night with Luke. He'd taken her to the boardwalk, and even though she'd been there on countless other occasions over the years, walking it with him had been… different. Over the past couple of months, she'd been grateful for his friendship, not to mention the countless ways he'd helped her get her business off the ground, but somewhere along the way, she'd begun to see him in a new light.

And she had to admit, it was nice to feel the excitement of a prospective romance again. She'd dated sporadically over the years but had never met someone special… or someone who had stacked up to Jax, her first—and truthfully, only—love. Their breakup had been brutal to her young heart, but they had recently reconnected as friends, and she had even begun letting him back into her life. Cautiously, of course. That wasn't a door she wanted to open fully yet, but at this point, she didn't go into panic mode every time she saw his face—a solid accomplishment on her part.

If only she could stop herself from thinking about him. His face was always there, lurking in the corner of her mind, a stark reminder of the love she had lost so long ago. For years, she had blamed herself, and him, but when he recently admitted to her the truth about that long-ago summer, she began to understand that neither one of them was responsible for what had happened, and both had suffered greatly from it.

That was little consolation. Still, it was something.

A knock on the door interrupted her thoughts, and Daphne gave the cake she was practicing on one last critical look before setting down her piping bag and wiping her icing-streaked hands on her apron. She glanced through the peephole before answering, glad to see her best friend Tana on the other side of the door, though she did her best to ignore the nagging sense of disappointment she felt when she realized that Jax wasn't with her. And why would he be? For both their sakes, they were keeping a healthy distance from each other.

She flung open the door to greet her friend, then saw, to her surprise, that Tana was accompanied by a young woman with dark hair, a delicate-featured face, and a bright smile. She wore a colorful tunic over stylish white leggings, and if Daphne had ever worn those gold wedge sandals for one of her shifts at the diner, she'd be crying uncle before the first of her shift's appetizers were delivered.

"Daphne," Tana said, wrapping an arm around the young woman's shoulders, "I'd love for you to meet my daughter, Emery. She's on break for a few weeks and decided to visit the island to see the inn and meet the whole gang. Emery, this is Daphne, one of my oldest and dearest friends."

"I've heard so many stories about you," Emery said, her eyes lighting up as the two women shook hands. "I can't tell you how many times my mother told me the story about the time the two of you snuck a fake jellyfish into Uncle Jax's beach bag."

"He almost had a heart attack on the spot," Tana said, grinning at Daphne as both women burst into laughter at the memory. "Do you remember how high-pitched his scream was? We imitated him for the rest of that summer. I swear, by the time we took the ferry back to the mainland to start the school year, I thought he was never going to speak to me again."

Then the light dimmed from her smile as she realized the topic of conversation and shot Daphne an apologetic look—since learning about Daphne and Jax's past, Tana had been careful to tiptoe around the subject of her brother whenever Daphne was present.

"It's okay, it's a good memory," Daphne said with a dismissive wave of her hand as Emery watched the two women curiously. Then, to cover the awkward moment, she opened the door wider and ushered Tana and her daughter inside. "You picked the right time to visit—I have five terribly decorated wedding cakes just begging for someone to eat them and put them out of their misery. They might look like they've been through the wringer, but I promise, they'll taste better than that."

She led her guests into the kitchen, then lifted one of the cakes from the counter and carried it to her small table as Tana and Emery chose seats. Then she slid the knife through the bottom tier, cutting generous portions of the red velvet cake for each of them as Tana filled her in on Emery's surprise visit. "And you got to meet Reed, I assume?" Daphne asked, sliding into the seat beside Emery and grabbing a fork.

Emery nodded through a mouthful of cake, then swallowed and said, "I certainly did," with a sly look at her mother.

"What?" Tana set down her own fork with a frown. "I thought you liked Reed."

"I do." Emery nodded fervently. "But when you told me over the phone that you were dating someone, I sort of expected him to be, well... old." She gave a nonchalant shrug and dug back into her slice of cake as Tana shot a look of horror at Daphne, who quickly covered the smile threatening to form on her lips.

"Care to share what you mean by that?" Tana folded her arms across her chest and gave her a severe look, though Daphne could tell by the gleam in her eye that she was amused by her daughter's observation.

Emery shrugged. "He's hot. Even with the gray in his hair."

Tana rested her forehead against the table with a groan while Daphne's eyes flooded with tears of laughter and Emery looked between the two of them, brow furrowed in confusion. "What?"

"Nothing." Tana patted her hand affectionately. "Absolutely nothing. I'm glad you approve—and for the record, I'm not ready to put both feet in the grave just yet. You'll have to save the motorized scooter for a Christmas present for another year."

"Too bad." Emery grinned at her and flipped her long, dark hair over her shoulders. "I've been saving my money all year to buy you the best one on the market."

The playful banter continued for another few minutes as the women enjoyed their cake—Emery and Tana lavished praise on Daphne's baking skills, both requesting another large slice that they dug into with vigor—until Tana directed her attention to Daphne during a lull in the conversation when Emery stepped outside to take a phone call. "So tell me—how was your date with Luke?"

"It was…" Daphne pursed her lips as she searched for the right word to describe the evening. "Surprising, I guess you could say."

Tana's eyebrows rose. "How so?"

Daphne leaned back in her chair with a sigh. "We had a nice time. A *really* nice time. Not that I expected we wouldn't—it's just…" She shook her head. "I don't know, everyone seems to think that Luke is still hung up on his ex-wife, but he was so attentive, so engaged, throughout our entire date. He was the perfect gentleman, and not for one second did I think his mind was elsewhere."

She shrugged and ran a hand through her shoulder-length blonde hair. "I could be wrong, though. It's not like I was going to say to him, 'Hey, Luke, why in the world are you out on a date with me when the entire world thinks you're still in love with Lydia? And oh, by the way, are you sure you even remember my name?'" She smiled wryly.

"Luke's a hard man to read," Tana said, cupping her chin as she stared out the kitchen window in thought. "From what Reed's told me, he took the divorce really hard. But that doesn't mean he's not ready to put himself out there again—and why not with you?" She reached over to cover Daphne's hand with her own. Then she sighed. "I heard they were together from the time they were teenagers. And we never really do forget our first love, do we?"

"No," Daphne said quietly, her mind automatically drifting toward Jax once more. "I guess we don't."

Tana searched her friend's face for several long moments as the silence stretched between them. "I've always been a big believer in second chances," she finally said, her eyes still on Daphne. "And if it seems like he's ready… he just may be."

Five minutes later, after Tana and Emery had said goodbye and left Daphne alone in her kitchen once more, she was still trying to work out whether Tana had been referring to Luke... or someone else entirely.

CHAPTER 5

A few blocks down the road, Jax Keller dabbed his sweat-streaked face with a dish towel and slung it over his shoulder, then stepped back to inspect his handiwork. The inn's large kitchen countertops were lined with plate after plate of breakfast fare—stacks of bananas foster pancakes, strawberry waffles with homemade whipped cream, California-inspired egg and avocado burritos with mango salsa—and enough jugs of freshly squeezed fruit juice to quench the thirst of the entire Dolphin Bay tourist population in the dog days of August.

He had spent the past few weeks carefully crafting each plate, testing version after version until he was satisfied with the results. It was tedious, to be sure—but well worth it, too. During the inn's golden days, Bennet, Uncle Henry's chef, had served award-winning breakfasts to the guests each morning, and Jax was honored to follow in his footsteps.

Temporarily, at least. He had no plans to stay on the island in the long-term, but he had made a promise to Uncle Henry to oversee the inn's break-fast relaunch, and he would honor it to the best of his abilities. Tana was planning to unveil the inn's new website in two days, and even though they expected reservations to be modest at first with the summer tourist season soon coming to an end, Jax wanted to be prepared.

"What's all this?"

Uncle Henry had appeared in the doorway out of nowhere—how the old man managed to creep up on him so often with that cane of his, Jax had no idea, but his great-uncle's constant lurking around the inn had caused him to nearly jump out of his skin on more than one occasion.

"This," Jax said, gesturing to the plates lining the counter, "is your next breakfast menu." He grabbed a fork out of a nearby drawer and passed it to his uncle. "Go on. Try a bite of everything. In fact," he added, grabbing another fork and pulling out two chairs at the counter, "I think I'll join you."

Uncle Henry was quiet for a long moment, remaining rooted to the spot, leaving Jax awkwardly holding two forks and grinning like an idiot. The smile slipped from his lips as Henry limped forward, using his cane for support, and gazed down at the plates, his mouth pursed as if he'd never seen food quite like this before.

Frowning, Jax took a silent inventory of the dishes for what had to be the thousandth time over the past few weeks. Had he gone overboard with the creativity? He knew Uncle Henry would find the mango salsa to be a stretch—the man had eaten cold porridge with precisely seven slices of ripe banana every morning for as long as Jax could remember—but surely the waffles wouldn't get the ax?

"Is something wrong?" he asked, letting out a small, nervous laugh as he tried to calculate how long it would take him to develop and perfect an entirely new, entirely vanilla menu. Reaching one finger, he surreptitiously nudged the waffle plate to the left until it was front and center in his uncle's line of vision.

Henry bent down, as much as his cane would allow, and peered at the burrito, his bushy gray eyebrows furrowed in concentration, as though he were trying to solve a particularly complicated calculus problem. Then, without a word, he removed the fork from Jax's fingers, dipped the very tip of it into the salsa, and dabbed it on his tongue.

By now, Jax was holding his breath, his eyes glued to his uncle's face. After an excruciatingly long twenty seconds, the old man said, "Huh," then moved on to the waffles. While Jax waited, wondering why on earth he was more nervous than a contestant on a Gordon Ramsey cooking show, Henry thumped his way down the counter, sampling a bite from each dish. When he had finished—not saying a word in the process, or even giving any indication that he wasn't completely appalled by what he was eating— he thumped back toward Jax, clapped him on the shoulder, and said, "Well done."

Jax, whose face was twisted in an anticipatory wince, exhaled in surprise. "You're happy with it? If there's anything you'd like to add, I can—"

"No, this'll do just fine." Henry gave the dishes a last critical once-over, then grunted and grabbed the burrito, balancing it in one hand while gripping his cane with the other as he limped away.

Jax watched him leave, shaking his head and wondering how many decades of living by himself it had taken for the old man to lose every last one of his social skills, then he turned his attention back to the plates. He was just lifting the first well-deserved forkful of pancakes to his lips when his cell phone rang. Grumbling in annoyance, he set down his fork and slid the phone out of his pocket, checking the screen and seeing an unfamiliar number and area code.

"Jax Keller," he said, eyeing the stack of pancakes with regret before pushing them away.

"Mr. Keller, hello, my name is Steve Neuman. I'm a restaurant investor in Miami Beach. I'd like to speak with you for a few minutes, if you have the time."

"Sure, give me one second," Jax said, frowning as he tried to figure out what this man might want. He left the kitchen, nodding to Henry at the front desk —his great-uncle was currently elbow deep in his burrito and barely grunted a response—before stepping out onto the wraparound porch. It was his favorite spot at the inn, the place where he came to decompress, gather his thoughts, and plan for the future. He settled himself into one of the new rocking chairs and gazed out over the serene waters, today a deep blue that reflected the cloudless sky.

"Okay, go ahead," he said, bracing his feet on the

railing. "A Miami Beach restaurant investor, you say?"

"Yes, for twenty-five years," the man said modestly. "My team and I are behind some of the most popular spots in the city—El Dorado, The Diablo Grill, Hester's on the Beach." He rattled off the restaurants as if everyone had heard of them, though Jax hadn't the faintest clue what any of them were. He hadn't stepped foot in Florida a day in his life, spending all of his twenties and thirties holed up in kitchens along the Eastern Seaboard, honing his craft.

"Anyway," the man continued after dropping a few more names, "we're opening a new bistro called Thistle & Thyme, and we're looking for the right chef to run it. A buddy of mine visited your restaurant in Philly, and he suggested I get in touch. According to him, your food's out of this world."

"Thank you," Jax said, quietly accepting the compliment, which felt good to hear after his entire life had recently crashed and burned so thoroughly. He'd been hiding away at the inn since then, licking his wounds and trying not to think about all he had lost—successfully, for the most part. He hoped whatever the man had to say wasn't about to squash the tenuous grip he had on peace right now.

"Anyway, I'm sure you're a busy man, so I'll cut to the chase." Steve cleared his throat. "We're looking for a top-notch chef for our new restaurant—it's in a prime location, right in the middle of the city's nightlife scene. We're inviting a handful of chefs from around the country to come check us out, cook a few dishes, see if they're a good fit. I'll be honest with you, though—we've checked you out, read up on your accomplishments, and that, along with my guy's personal recommendation... well, you're our top candidate. So would you be interested?"

Jax was quiet for a long moment, trying to wrap his mind around the sudden turn of events. Here he was, minding his own business, working hard to convince a grumpy eighty-three-year-old man who lived on an island quite literally in the middle of nowhere to sign off on a plate of pancakes—quite possibly the easiest dish he'd thrown together in a good twenty years—when out of the blue, a man he'd never even heard of decided to give him a chance most chefs would kill for?

There was a catch. There had to be.

Steve cleared his throat again, then filled the void in the conversation with a chuckle. "Anyone there?"

"Yes. Sorry." Jax straightened up in his chair and ran his hand through his hair, making it stand on end. A feeling of excitement was welling up inside him, along with something else, something he couldn't quite identify but felt a lot like… regret?

Huh. He'd have to unpack that one later.

"I'm definitely interested," he continued, already mentally running through a list of his best recipes. "When do you want me to come out?"

"Well, things are moving at warp speed down here—when we set our sights on something, we get it done. We've already interviewed a couple of guys, and we're looking to make our final selection by the end of the month. I'll be out of town this weekend, so how about the weekend after that? Can you fly here for a couple of days and see what we have to offer?"

There it was. The catch. Jax felt his heart sinking in disappointment as he glanced over his shoulder at the inn—and inside, Uncle Henry, now finished with his burrito and perusing a handful of paperwork, studying it over the top of his glasses.

"I'm sorry, I can't," Jax said, scarcely able to believe the words coming out of his own mouth. He closed his eyes and shook his head. "I've committed to helping a family member run his inn's kitchen for a couple of months, and he's reopening for business in a few short days. We have to plan for last-minute bookings, and right now, I'm the only chef he's got. I made a commitment, and I have to honor it." Those last words were bitter, and Jax swallowed hard in a vain attempt to banish them.

Steve was silent for a long moment, and then he said, "You know what? I've been going full-steam for months now, and I could use a break. Why don't you give me the details of where you're at, and I'll come to you. I can sample your food and take my wife on a vacation—kill two birds with one stone and make myself look like husband of the year. You know what they say: happy wife, happy life." He laughed while Jax tightened his grip on the phone, still trying to work out whether this was all someone's idea of a joke.

Fifteen minutes later, after hearing more details of Steve Neuman's new restaurant venture—not to mention a long list of his credentials in the industry, which were enough to make Jax's head spin—he decided that it was not, in fact, a joke.

It was the opportunity of a lifetime.

HENRY TURNER HEAVED a long sigh as he settled himself into his seat on the Dolphin Bay ferry with a quick nod to Kurt, the captain, perched behind the wheel. He hadn't been on the ferry alone in months, thanks to the lingering mobility issues he'd been having in the aftermath of his stroke, and he'd made it a point not to tell Tana that he was leaving the island for a short while—knowing her, she'd get herself in a complete tizzy about him traveling alone and insist on coming with him. Which, right now, was the absolute last thing he wanted.

For some things, a man needed privacy.

He had to admit, having his great-niece at the inn hadn't been nearly as bad as he'd feared. While she had a habit of sticking her nose into his business—and grinning at him and Edie like they were hormonal teenagers every time she caught them walking hand-in-hand through the inn's hallways—he was starting to actually enjoy her company. And if he was in the habit of making admissions to himself these days, he also knew he owed Tana, big-time, for helping to bring the two of them together. Edie was the only person in the world he had truly let into his heart since the days of his youth. She was the bright spot in his day, the song in his heart.

He could only dare to hope she felt the same way. Soon, he'd find out.

As the ferry chugged away from the harbor, cutting a clean path through the gentle, white-capped waves, Henry settled back in his seat, cane propped at his side, and closed his eyes, allowing the sun's warm rays to play across his face. Thankfully, his fellow passengers were few and far between, and no one had decided to sit next to him and insist on making awkward small-talk for the duration of the trip.

If there was one thing he hated, it was—

Stop that, you old kook. He could hear Edie's voice in his head as clearly as if she were sitting next to him, and he opened his eyes and glanced at the empty chair beside him, just in case. She'd been on his case recently about learning to become more sociable, insisting that he practice every time they were out and about in town together, ignoring his grumblings that the best kind of company was a book, a cup of hot tea, and a good view of the sea.

And he stood by that, too. But the truth was, he'd do anything for her.

The ferry ride passed more quickly than he would have liked, and before he knew it, Henry was giving Kurt a goodbye nod and heading down the ferry's ramp, feeling slightly unsteady as his feet touched solid ground. He wobbled for a moment but regained his footing, although, to his chagrin, he noticed more than a few passersby preparing to launch forward to rescue him. So it was with an embarrassed flush to his cheeks that he made his way down the sidewalk, heading toward the same small shop on the shoreline that had been standing there the last time he had visited, sixty-five years ago.

The gentleman who used to run the shop had passed away long ago, but the name on the sign hanging above the door remained the same—a son, he supposed, or maybe even a grandson. My good-ness, he thought with a shake of his head; how had the years passed so quickly?

He paused for a moment before entering the shop, his hand on the doorknob as he remembered that long-ago day when he'd last been here, a boy on the cusp of manhood, a boy who had no idea what the next few decades would bring. He'd loved, and lost, and loved again, but somehow, he'd made it through the years all right.

Now, he planned to make sure the years that remained were much, much better than all right.

"Good afternoon, sir," a young man in a crisp

gray suit said, glancing up from behind the counter as Henry finally entered the shop. "How can I help you today?"

Remembering Edie's admonishments, Henry gave the man as bright a smile as he could muster. "I'm looking for an engagement ring."

CHAPTER 6

he line for the ferry was scant; other than a couple of teenagers with beach bags and boogie boards, and an older man leaning on a cane, a gift bag from the nearby jewelry store dangling from his wrist, Lydia was completely alone. Thankfully—for her sanity as well as that of everyone else around her, including any passing dolphins—Maura and her family had chartered a private helicopter to Dolphin Bay and would be arriving first thing tomorrow morning. That gave Lydia just enough time to gather her wits and prepare for what was sure to be three of the hardest days of her life.

Her mother's words had been ringing in her head since last night, making sleep impossible; instead,

Lydia had spent the endless hours of the night staring at the ceiling in the darkness, a reel of her life with Luke playing through her head. The first day they met, in high school study hall—he'd grabbed her homework and spun it around to find out her name, his smile mischievous but his voice warm as they spent the rest of the period talking, like no one else was in the room. Their first kiss, behind the bleachers at the homecoming football game—Luke, the star football player beloved by all the girls; Lydia, the editor of the school newspaper, most at ease with herself when she was sitting behind her computer, the words pouring out of her. The day he asked her to be his wife—while sitting together in the shadows of the island's magnificent lighthouse, watching the sun set over a gently rolling ocean.

The first few years of their life together were magical, and as their twenties ticked into their thirties, they began to have the same conversation as countless couples everywhere: when to add children to their family.

Who could have known that would be their undoing?

Lydia stared down at the ground, willing away the memories, as the ferry glided into the harbor and the captain lowered the ramp. She entered the short line behind the elderly gentleman with the cane, and it was only when she registered his face for the first time that she realized he was Henry Turner, the man who owned Dolphin Bay's oldest and most recognizable inn. He was whistling—actually *whistling*—and that alone caught Lydia off-guard; Old Man Turner, as they called him in her high school days, was an unfriendly, oftentimes downright unpleasant man the islanders knew to steer clear of.

At least, that's what he used to be. Now, as Lydia watched him swing the jewelry bag back and forth from the hand not clutching the cane, she realized that there was something about his features… a new lightness, perhaps, that made him look ten years younger than the last time she'd seen him.

A car horn honked behind her, and Lydia turned automatically, watching as a pickup and a bicycle barely avoided a collision, and when she swung back around, she saw that Henry had turned too—and now, their gazes snagged. His faded green eyes widened slightly in recognition, and then he gave her a pleasant nod before returning his attention to the ferry, where the captain was now beckoning the small group of riders to board.

Lydia exhaled softly, though she hadn't even realized she'd been holding her breath. She was glad

Henry hadn't tried to strike up a conversation, not that she'd expected him to—they'd lived on the same island for most of Lydia's life and had never said a word to each other, even when a seven-year-old Lydia had knocked on the inn's front door with a box of candy for her elementary school fundraiser. When he opened the door, his usual grumpy expression had turned positively foul, and he shut it again without another word. Her mother had spent the next few minutes comforting her, explaining to her teary-eyed daughter that he simply preferred to be left alone, and that his rudeness wasn't personal. Since then, she'd given him a wide berth.

But that long-ago encounter wasn't why she wanted to give him an even wider berth right now. She'd heard through the grapevine that Henry's inn was undergoing a massive renovation, with Luke scoring the job—which was well-deserved, of course, given his talent and dedication to his business. If she struck up a conversation with Henry, he could very well invite her to see the inn, which was laughable, of course, but stranger things had happened—like Lydia suddenly finding herself on the island she had fled five years ago, with no plans of returning.

And she couldn't go back to that inn. Not now, not ever.

She knew she had to see Luke, had known it from the moment she picked up the phone all those weeks ago to warn him she was coming to Dolphin Bay. She just wanted it to be on her own terms.

With that in mind, Lydia grabbed her suitcase, forced one foot in front of the other, and boarded the ferry.

She was going home.

"I DON'T EVEN KNOW what to say. Thank you. Thank you so much." Tana removed a tissue from her pocket and dabbed at her eyes, then shook her head and laughed. "You must think I'm being ridiculous for crying. It's just… when I came back to the island and saw the inn for the first time in so many years, I could barely believe my own eyes. But now, the transformation… it's amazing." She blew her nose, then laughed again. "I feel like I've spent most of the past two days weeping, I'm so happy."

She wiped her eyes once more, then balled the tissue up in her fist and smiled at Luke. "You've been wonderful to work with, and I know I speak for my uncle too when I say that if you ever need a recommendation, a review, anything—please, don't hesitate to call."

"It was my pleasure," Luke said, and meant it. Even though his job could be grueling at times, he lived for the moments when his clients saw the full effect of his work for the first time. And he had to admit, the Inn at Dolphin Bay was some of his best work to date—he'd poured his heart and soul into the job, knowing that the inn was an important landmark on the island, a place where families had been coming to enjoy all that Dolphin Bay had to offer for decades.

The inn meant something to the people who lived here.

It meant something even more to Luke.

"Like this room," Tana was saying in awe as she opened the door to the largest guest room on the second floor, which boasted magnificent views of the Dolphin Bay coastline, with the mainland a hazy purple outline just visible in the distance. Luke caught a glimpse of the ferry chugging to shore, cutting a clean line through the water and leaving a churning froth of white-capped waves in its wake. He focused his attention on the ferry, glad for the distraction. He probably should have been listening to Tana, who was still lavishing praise on him as she walked around the newly renovated room, her fingers trailing along the walls, which were painted in a soft sea-green color that Luke had personally selected.

But right now, he needed to be looking anywhere, *anywhere*, but at this room. Working in it had been bad enough, but at least when he was on the job he had something else to focus on. That way, he wouldn't find himself hurtled back into the memories of the night he and Lydia had stayed in this very room, Luke carrying his new wife over the threshold, her beautiful white gown trailing on the carpet behind them… and then him accidentally stepping on her gown and sending them both tumbling to the floor.

Oh, how they'd laughed then—the kind of impossible-to-catch-your-breath belly laughs that had tears pouring from their eyes as they clutched their stomachs and tried to breathe.

He'd never known happiness like that night.

Luke kept his eyes glued to a pair of seagulls circling the shoreline, their gray-tipped wings spread wide, their white feathers catching the glint of the unforgiving sun, high in the summer sky. Tana was still talking, he supposed, but by now, he had abandoned all pretenses of listening. He didn't register the silence until a soft hand on his arm startled him out of his thoughts, and it was with regret that he turned from the peaceful ocean vista and focused his attention on his client—and now, his friend.

"Is today the day?" she asked, her voice gentle, her brown eyes warm with concern.

Luke swallowed hard and nodded. "It is."

He had grown close with Tana since she and Reed had begun dating, the three of them often meeting for lunch or a late dinner, once Luke and his crew had packed up at the inn for the evening. On one of those occasions, he had confided in them about Lydia's phone call, the news that she would be returning to the island for a single weekend. Neither had brought it up since then, but Tana squeezed his hand as she led him out of the room—thankfully—and down the steps to the inn's parlor.

This room, too, was transformed, with a butter-soft leather couch and pair of reclining chairs in the softest shade of blue, a new throw rug with a swirling pattern of tan and blue that was reminiscent of the seashore, and bookcases stuffed with novels for the inn's guests to enjoy. Tana sat in one chair while Luke sat in another, grateful once more to be out of that suffocating room.

When Tana turned to him, ready to speak, he expected her to ask about Lydia, and how he was feeling about her impending arrival. Instead, she said, "A few days ago, I found out that Derek is engaged to the woman he cheated on me with."

Although the words were shocking, and made Luke shake his head in sympathy, she said them as though she were merely reporting on the weather. Tana had handled the recent uprooting of her life with grace, which was something Luke would always admire about her. When Lydia left him, he was a shell of a man for months.

Years, actually.

Luke sighed to himself. Actually, he had never recovered, which became all too clear to him the moment he heard her voice again.

"I'm sorry," he said quietly as Tana made herself comfortable in the chair and crossed one leg over the other. "How are you doing?"

She gazed out the window for a long moment, watching a family with young children head down the path to the beach, laughing and chatting as they lugged a cooler, beach chairs, and enough sand toys to keep an entire kindergarten class busy for weeks.

When they rounded a bend on the dirt trail and disappeared from view amidst the tall dune grass blowing gently in the breeze kicked up from the water, she turned back to him with a smile.

"I'm doing okay. I was shocked at first, of course —I didn't want to talk about it, not even to Reed. But that night, when I had a chance to sit with the news… just sit with it and take it all in… I realized that I was semi-okay."

She leaned forward to rest a comforting hand on his knee. "I'm telling you this because when I was in the midst of everything, when my life was quite literally falling apart before my eyes, I never thought I'd be able to accept this kind of news with some measure of peace. But I've grown since then, I've started a new life that I'm excited about, and that's made it all okay."

She laughed and tucked a strand of her dark hair behind her ear. "Not that I'm about to be a guest on the big day, mind you, but I'm also not going to spend it holed up in a dark room eating buckets of ice cream and crying over my wedding photos." Tana gave his knee a light squeeze. "What I'm trying to say is that if and when you do see Lydia, you might just surprise yourself—you might be okay too."

Luke considered her words for a long moment as

he gazed down at his left hand. For months after she had left, when he had finally slid the wedding ring from his finger, a tan line remained, a constant reminder of all that he had lost. Even now, he sometimes reached for it in the mornings on autopilot as he prepared to start his day, groping around on his nightstand for the small velvet box that was no longer there.

"She never even told me she was leaving." He glanced up and caught Tana's gaze. "Did I ever tell you that? The last time I saw her, she was sitting at the kitchen table, drinking coffee and eating a bowl of cereal like she did every other morning of our marriage. Before I left for work, I told her I'd see her later that evening, and I gave her a kiss on the cheek —" He swallowed hard, closing his eyes against the memory that still stung him to his core. "I never imagined that would be our last goodbye."

Tana fell silent then, her grip on his knee loosening, as though she were lost in another world. A little while later, she said, "I didn't know that. It must have been awful for you. I know what it's like to have your entire world turned upside down without notice, and Lydia should be ashamed of herself."

"In some ways, she should," Luke said, leaning his head against the soft leather of the chair and letting out a long sigh. "And in other ways, I understand why she did what she did. We were… in a bad place. A dark place. I always thought we'd come out of it stronger, but Lydia… everything here, on this island… and with me…" His voice lowered to a whisper. "It was a constant reminder, and she couldn't bear it anymore."

He thought back to those grief-stricken days, to hearing the doctor say, once again, the words that shattered them: "I'm sorry. There's no heartbeat."

How many had they lost? Over the years, Luke had forced himself to lose count. Upwards of a dozen, before they finally decided they couldn't go through the agony of hope and the heartbreak of despair one more time. Lydia took the loss of motherhood hard—so hard, in fact, that after the last time, she was unable to get out of bed for a month. And when she finally did, things between them were never the same.

And Luke hadn't expected that they would be. Still, he wanted to walk the road to recovery—some semblance of it, at least—together, hand in hand, her head on his shoulder, his arm around her waist. They would move on, forge a happy life together—a different life, no doubt, but he was confident that what they had would overcome anything.

In the end, it hadn't. The pain had been too much, and they had navigated it by turning away from each other, by taking separate paths on the long and winding road to peace.

Luke was still walking that path; would, perhaps, always be walking it. He suspected Lydia would as well.

"So do you want to see her?" Tana's voice broke through the silence, and Luke took several deep breaths, pulling himself out of the memories he had tried so hard to force into the furthest corners of his mind. He looked at Tana but didn't really see her; instead, he saw the girl with the golden hair and the sunny smile who had captured his heart when he was still just a boy, who had captured his heart still when the world they built together was crumbling at their feet.

"Yes," he said, his voice soft. "I very much do."

CHAPTER 7

"*H*ey, where are you off to?" Jax asked, shuffling up to Tana, who was leaning against the inn's front desk, her phone in one hand, purse in the other. She jumped guiltily and tried to discreetly slide her phone back into her pocket, but her older brother was having none of it.

"Give it here," he said, beckoning to her with a stern expression. He glanced at the screen, nodded in confirmation, and sighed as he closed the Internet tab Tana had been reading. "Honestly, sis, why are you doing this to yourself? I'm starting to think you're a masochist."

"Yeah, well, you would be too if the news of your ex's engagement—before the two of you even got divorced, mind you—was splashed all over TMZ and

Page Six. It's humiliating." She shook her head, then ran both hands through her hair in frustration. "Remember how quiet I was as a kid? Never in a million years would I think my dirty laundry would be aired for the entire country to see. I didn't ask for this, you know."

"I know," Jax said quietly, reaching over and dropping the phone into her purse. "Have you talked to him about it?"

Tana stared at her brother in horror, certain she had misunderstood. "Talked to Reed?" she clarified.

"No, talked to Derek." Jax shrugged, shoving his hands deep into the pockets of his jeans. "You know, give him a call and have it out with him. Say all the things you need to say so you can find closure."

"I have closure," Tana said defensively, sliding her feet into her sandals and hitching her purse over her shoulder, hoping Jax would take the hint and stop this conversation before they got any further down the rabbit hole. "When I went back to California to pack up the house, we said goodbye to each other. Sort of." She thought back to that night, when Derek had taken her by surprise and shown up at their house unannounced, Lucia in tow.

"Goodbye isn't good riddance," Jax said, lightly grabbing her arm to prevent her from leaving. "After all he's done to you, all the embarrassment you've endured, and are *still* enduring because of him"—he nodded to Tana's phone—"don't you think you deserve a chance to speak your mind, once and for all?"

Tana stared at her brother without really seeing him as she imagined what it would feel like to confront Derek. Jax was right—she'd never really said her piece. She'd been too shocked and heartsick in the aftermath of discovering Derek's affair to do more than curl up under the covers and pray it was nothing but an awful dream, and since then, she'd done everything she could to avoid him. All communication was currently done through their divorce lawyers, and whatever scraps of information Emery let slip. As far as Tana was concerned, that was just fine—the idea of facing him again, even over the phone, was more than she was willing to endure.

"That's not really my style." Tana shrugged and turned toward the front door. "Yelling at him, or whatever you're envisioning I do, isn't going to change the past. He can have his engagement. I'll take my dignity. Now if you'll excuse me, Daphne asked me to stop by the bakery and see how everything's coming together, and I don't want to keep her waiting."

With that, she slung her purse over her shoulder and opened the door, but before she could put one foot out, Jax was beside her again. "Do you mind if I tag along? I'd love to see the place." His eager tone gave her pause, and she gave her brother an odd look.

"What?" He laughed. "I need a change of scenery. I've spent the past few weeks practically living in the inn's kitchen, testing and re-testing recipes until I want to tear the entire oven off the wall and toss it into the ocean. So you could say that it's starting to wear on me. Besides, I want to show Daphne my support. I'm excited for her. Back when we were kids, she used to talk about opening up her own bakery all the time—and it's great to see her going for it."

Tana winced automatically at the mention of Jax and Daphne's shared past, but she quickly tried to cover it—not quickly enough, though, because Jax saw her expression and shook his head. "We're trying to build a friendship, and this is one step closer to that." He joined Tana in stepping out onto the inn's porch, and despite her reservations that Jax's presence in the bakery was just about the last thing Daphne would want, they set off down the cobblestone sidewalk and headed toward town.

The sun was just beginning to drop below the horizon as they walked side by side, dodging the groups of tourists headed out for dinner or the boardwalk and waving to the townspeople they passed, many of them closing up their shops for the evening. As they passed Edie's antique store, Tana glanced in automatically, and grinned to herself as she saw Henry leaning against the counter, deep in conversation with his sweetheart, both of them wearing soft smiles.

Her uncle had been spending more and more time with Edie as of late, and Tana knew without asking that the relationship was growing serious. According to Reed, his sisters initially had a difficult time accepting the news that Edie was dating Henry —which was fair, Tana thought, given his decades-long reputation as a grouch—but seeing their mother's obvious happiness had helped change their minds. As far as Tana was concerned, the two of them were an inspiration, a real-life example that the door should never be closed on love.

Jax was staring at the older couple too, a slight furrow in his brow, and when Tana caught his gaze, she thought she saw a hint of sadness reflected in it. "Everything okay?" she asked as they rounded the corner, leaving the antique shop behind.

Her brother hesitated for a moment, his gaze flicking out to the sea and then back again. He shrugged casually, but Tana wasn't fooled by the would-be nonchalant gesture. She stopped walking, catching his arm so that he did the same, and waited patiently for him to speak.

"I don't know," he said, blowing out a breath and running a hand through his dark hair. "Seeing them together, happy… I guess it brings up a lot of stuff for me."

Tana raised one eyebrow. "'Stuff' as in Daphne?" Despite her brother's protests—and Daphne's refusal to speak on the subject—Tana was having a hard time believing that they could truly be friends. Nor was she certain they wanted to be just that. She saw the look of longing in their eyes each time the other was mentioned, let alone the chemistry that was almost palpable in the air whenever they were in the same room.

Jax gave her a stern look. "*Stuff* as in love. Relationships. Family. I always thought I'd be married, have someone by my side as I grew older. I guess life has a funny way of turning out how you least expect it. Like this." He waved his arm in a semi-circle, encompassing the island's town square and the stunning ocean scenery beyond. "Did you ever think either one of us would be back in Dolphin Bay, let alone *both* of us?" He laughed. "How did we get here?"

"I have no idea," Tana said, her eyes going to the rapidly setting sun. She began walking again, quicker this time, eager to reach their destination. Daphne's stress level was through the roof right now —understandably, of course, given the mounting pressures that came with quitting her job and throwing every last dime she had into starting a new business venture. She'd been eager for Tana to see the bakery, and the last thing Tana wanted was for Daphne to think she'd forgotten. She needed support, and Tana was more than happy to give it. It was the least she could do for the person who had been by her side the most as she recovered from Derek's affair, and the fallout from the end of her marriage.

As they walked, Tana glanced at Jax, who had hurried forward to match her pace. "Want to talk about it?" Her brother wasn't one to share his feelings, so this type of conversation was new territory for them both.

"There's nothing to talk about," Jax said with a wave of his hand as they rounded the corner and the bakery came into view. "I'm just musing, that's all. I haven't had free time in years, so I've had plenty of opportunities lately to think about the state of my life, how I want the future to look."

"And?" Tana asked, glancing sideways at her brother. "What does that future look like?"

He gave her his trademark grin, his eyes crinkling with laughter. "I have no idea. If you want, you can figure it out for me."

"Don't tempt me," she teased with a wave of her finger. "If I had a say in things, you'd stay right here, on the island, and be with—" She stopped abruptly, realizing what she'd been about to say, and pressed her lips together.

Jax gave her a curious look. "Be with who?"

"Me." Tana linked her arm through his as they approached the bakery's entrance. "I've missed you all these years, and I'm glad to be spending time with you again. No matter how old a girl gets, she always needs her big brother. Her much, *much* older big brother."

Jax shot her an annoyed look as they both stopped outside the newly erected awning, a cheerful yellow and white pattern that immediately put a smile on Tana's face. "This looks great!" she said as she peered up at the lettering on the sign Daphne had commissioned that now hung above the awning. She'd agonized over the bakery's name for weeks before finally landing on Sugarbloom, and Tana felt her heart swelling with pride for her friend as she saw it in print for the first time.

Since Daphne had quit her job at Sal's, she'd finally stopped leaving the bakery windows shuttered during the day, and a quick peek inside revealed her standing behind the counter. Her back was to them as she studied something beside the cash register, giving Tana an opportunity to glance around the bakery's interior. And she was amazed by what she saw—Daphne had outdone herself with a modern yet cozy design, complete with cheerful white table and chair sets for customers to enjoy their desserts in-house while overlooking the island's beautiful coastline, a gleaming counter space and bakery case that would soon be filled with Daphne's incredible treats, and a wall lined with stunning paintings of the island, all created by local artists. All in all, the effect was magical.

Daphne turned around in surprise when Tana practically barreled through the door, Jax on her heels. "You did it," she cried, making a beeline for her friend. When she reached Daphne, she pulled her into a tight hug. "I'm so proud of you, Daph. You're really making it happen. None of what you told me does the bakery justice—it's gorgeous. It's absolutely gorgeous." She released Daphne from the hug, and her friend grinned at her, her eyes lit up with a happiness that Tana had never seen in them before.

"Thank you so much, I can't believe it's—" Daphne's voice faltered when she caught sight of Jax, hovering awkwardly in the background, but she immediately recovered, turning her attention back to Tana. "I can't believe it's all finally coming together. Which sounds silly, since it's only been a few months… I never could have done all of this as fast as I did without Luke's help."

She smiled softly at the mention of his name, and Tana's heart sank as the memory of the conversation she'd had with him earlier that day came flooding back. After he left, Tana had resolved to speak with Daphne about what she had seen in Luke's eyes as the conversation turned to his former wife, but now was not the time for that.

Now was the time for celebrating all of Daphne's accomplishments.

"What do you think?" Daphne asked, stepping around Tana to address Jax. He'd been standing off to the side, studying one of the landscape paintings of the Dolphin Bay harbor at sunset, his hands shoved in his pockets, the way they always were when he was uncomfortable. Tana stepped back, intent on watching their interaction, her eyes cutting back and forth between the two.

When Jax turned around, his gaze immediately snagged on Daphne, and he gave her a smile that lit up his whole face. "I think it's amazing." He stepped forward, his eyes still on hers, and pulled her into a long, tight hug. "I'm so proud of you, Daphne," he murmured into her hair.

Tana saw her friend stiffen at Jax's approach, but the moment his arms were around her, her entire body seemed to soften under his touch. Their embrace lingered for a few seconds longer than Tana would have expected, but when they finally pulled away from each other, Daphne immediately side-stepped him, returning to her place behind the counter, her expression blank.

"Thank you," she said in a businesslike tone. "It's been a hard few months, and I'm having a difficult time believing that I'll be open for business in a little more than a week. Hey," she added suddenly, her gaze returning to Jax. "Can I ask you something about your process for working with suppliers? How did you—"

Tana wandered away from the counter as the two of them began to talk shop, admiring the paintings lining the wall before drifting over to the window. The sun was almost fully set now, leaving a coral-streaked purple sky in its wake, the first hint of stars beginning to twinkle overhead. Her thoughts turned briefly to Luke; she wondered whether he'd run into Lydia yet. Dolphin Bay was a small island, not a place to visit if you didn't want to see and be seen. She glanced back at Daphne, who was now talking earnestly with Jax, both leaning casually against the counter, elbows propped on its surface. The last thing she wanted was to see her friend get hurt, and even though Daphne hadn't shared many details about her budding relationship with Luke, falling for a man who was already in love with someone else? No good could come of that.

Tana was still standing at the window a few minutes later when she caught sight of a familiar figure on the corner, leaning up against a lamppost that had just flicked on against the darkening sky. Her daughter's hair was cascading over her face, blocking it from view, but Tana would recognize her anywhere. She smiled as she watched her, flickering in and out of view amid the pedestrians strolling through town, and when Emery turned her way, Tana realized she was on the phone.

And she was crying.

Tana straightened up and headed for the door without a second thought, then stopped herself as Emery ended the call, looked at the phone for several long moments, and then slid it into her purse. She looked up, and Tana ducked out of the way—she didn't want her daughter to think she was snooping. Emery glanced around and then joined the foot traffic, wiping her eyes as she headed down the street… and straight for Daphne's bakery.

"Mom!" she said in surprise as Tana stepped out of the doorway in time to intercept her daughter as she walked past. Frowning, Emery looked up at the sign hanging above the bakery's door. "What are you doing here?" Then she peered inside the window and caught sight of Jax and Daphne, still at the counter, and her face lit up. "Is this Daphne's new bakery? She's told me so much about it—I've been dying to see it. Can I come in?"

No one but the most astute of observers—in other words, a mother—would have even recognized the hint of tears glistening at the corners of Emery's eyes, but Tana pretended not to notice as she ushered her daughter through the door. "I'm sure Daphne would love to show you around. She's just putting the finishing touches on the shop, and she'll be open for business in less than two weeks."

"And I'll be your first customer for sure," Emery said, gazing around in admiration. "This place is so chic, Daphne. It definitely wouldn't be out of place right in the middle of Manhattan." She greeted her uncle with a hug as Jax stepped away from Daphne.

"That's quite a compliment, thank you." Daphne grinned at Emery, then pressed her hands to her cheeks and shook her head in amazement as she looked around the shop. "It's funny, I didn't realize I actually had a sense of style until I started thinking about what kind of look I wanted to go for. That's what happens when you spend nearly three decades of your life in a greasy apron and sensible shoes."

The group chatted for a few more minutes, with Daphne proudly showing off the rest of the bakery, until she disappeared into the kitchen, returning a moment later with a plate of freshly baked chocolate chip cookies. "I know chocolate chip isn't fancy," she said apologetically as she set the plate down on a table near the window and the others gathered around. "But I also think it's important to keep the basics stocked."

"You always want a mix of new recipes and old favorites," Jax said, cookie halfway to his mouth. "When I had my restaurant, I worked around the clock trying to keep up with the latest trends in food. And do you know what I consistently sold the most of?" He took a bite of cookie and sighed happily. "A cheeseburger and fries." After polishing off the rest of his cookie, he said, "And on that note, I have news."

Tana and the others looked up at him expectantly as he took a deep breath and said, "I got a call from a restaurant investor the other day. He and his team have started a number of successful restaurants, and they're planning to open another one, a bistro, in a few months. One of his buddies heard of me, and they've invited me to apply for the position of head chef."

"Jax, that's wonderful!" Tana said, setting down her own cookie and throwing her arms around her brother. When she pulled back, she asked, "Where is it? The new bistro, that is."

"A prime spot, right on the water." Jax grinned at them. "In Miami Beach."

Emery and Tana shared looks of excitement before surrounding Jax, the three of them speaking over each other as they discussed this new—and very well-deserved—opportunity. Jax's entire face was lit up as he described the conversation he'd had with the investor, who'd be traveling to the island in a matter of weeks to sample his food. As soon as that happened, Tana knew, it would be a done deal. Jax's talent as a chef was known far and wide, and she couldn't be more thrilled for him.

Not until a few minutes later, when Tana heard the door to the bakery's kitchen close with a soft click, did she realize that Daphne was nowhere in sight.

CHAPTER 8

"*I* can't breathe! I think I'm going to have, like, an actual heart attack." Maura's voice was shrill to the point of being painful, and Lydia yanked the phone away from her ear with a wince. Maura and her entourage had arrived on Dolphin Bay a mere thirty minutes ago, yet Lydia had already been on the phone with her seven times.

The current crisis? One of the bridesmaids had decided to dye her hair blonde.

"It's not going to *match*!" Maura shrieked, causing Lydia to nudge the phone still further away; by now, it was practically across the room, not that any kind of distance would muffle the bride's rage. "I *specifically* picked out a pale yellow dress for her to wear since she was the only bridesmaid with dark hair. Now she's going to look like a banana." The last word came out as a wail, and Lydia had to slap a hand over her mouth to stop the snort of laughter threatening to escape.

Regaining her composure, she smoothed her voice into the professional yet soothing tone she always employed when dealing with a bride on the verge of a breakdown. "I know it's not what you envisioned, but I'm sure she'll look just fine. Besides, it's *your* day, Maura—everyone is going to be looking at you. Your dress is absolutely stunning, and I can promise you it'll be the talk of the town once the pictures are published in the society pages next week."

At those last words, Lydia shook her head. Who knew that actual society pages still existed? She did now, thanks to Maura's insistence that she contact every paper in the state with news of her impending nuptials. That only added to the enormous amount of pressure Lydia was under to make sure the day went off without a hitch, although the closer they got to the big moment, the more Lydia doubted this was what Maura actually wanted. Jared, her husband-to-be, always seemed like an afterthought, a footnote at his own wedding. Maura barely mentioned him, rarely asked his opinion, and other than a cursory introduction a few weeks into the wedding planning, Lydia had barely seen him.

But, Lydia reminded herself, that wasn't her concern right now. As long as he showed up and the wedding was a success, she had done her job. Her clients' personal lives were none of her business, though she always ended each event by wishing the new couple a long and happy marriage—and she truly meant it. Despite all that had happened in her life, Lydia believed in love, and happily-ever-afters, and soulmates.

Life is going to throw you all kinds of heartaches. Don't add losing your soulmate to the mix.

Lydia inhaled shakily as her mother's words echoed in her mind yet again. She'd been having a hard time shaking them off since her mother confronted her. They circled back to her each night, when the day's chaos was over and she was left with nothing but her thoughts as she sat alone in her apartment with a mug of cocoa and whatever Netflix show she could find that looked remotely interesting. Anything to pass the time. The nights were long, she'd discovered, when you no longer had anyone to share them with.

She exhaled, returning her attention to her client,

who had been silent this whole time as she considered Lydia's words. Finally, Maura sighed and said, "You're absolutely right, Lydia. Everyone *will* be looking at me, not her. If she wants to walk down the aisle with a terrible dye job and make a fool of herself in front of all my guests, that's on her. And on that note, were you able to get in touch with the editor of *Coastal Weddings*? She and Daddy are old friends, and she promised to send a reporter and photographer out to cover the wedding. Tell her I want the front page and a full spread or she can't put me in at all. Tell her—"

There was a rumble of voices in the background, followed by Maura saying, "Are you *kidding*, Jared? You were supposed to get a navy-blue tie, not a royal-blue one. Call the pilot *now* and have him fly you back to the mainland to exchange it. I don't care if he's got another passenger to pick up; this is more important. Daddy will cover the bill." Then, to Lydia, "Gotta go, another crisis to resolve. Call you soon. Muaaah."

Click.

Lydia dropped the phone into her lap and massaged her temples, trying to ward off the looming headache she had a feeling would be sticking around for the next few days. Then she kicked off her shoes and padded over to the window of her hotel room, tugging it up a few inches to let in the fresh sea air while she enjoyed the ocean view.

It was a glorious day on the island, and as Lydia caught a glimpse of a pair of dolphins leaping out of the water not far from the coastline, she let out a long sigh. She hadn't been back to Dolphin Bay in five years, and she missed it more than she could ever put into words. The island had been her home for almost her entire life; even after her parents had decided to move to the mainland so her father could be closer to work, Lydia had chosen to stay and build a life of her own here.

But Dolphin Bay was a small town, meaning it wasn't big enough for both her and Luke. One of them had to leave… and since she was the one who walked out the door, it was only fair that person was her. Still, the sea called to her; it was part of her soul, her place of peace and respite. Losing its constant, reassuring presence in her life had been one more blow she'd yet to fully come to terms with.

Lydia glanced at the clock on the nightstand. She had two hours of free time before she needed to head over to the venue to begin setting up, and she knew exactly how she was going to spend it. Grabbing her purse and sandals, she set her phone to silent—just for fifteen minutes, to clear her head, she reasoned—before opening her hotel room door and answering the call of the sea.

"I CAN'T BELIEVE it's finally here." Tana sat behind the inn's computer, her finger hovering over the mouse. "One more click and we'll be open for business." She turned to Reed, who was standing behind her, one hand on her shoulder. "Do you think anyone will come?"

"I do," he said confidently, waving toward the new website she'd spent weeks painstakingly constructing, with the help of Daphne and others. "You've got a professional site, guests can book their stay right online, and the pictures of the inn and the island are stunning—and they don't even do the place justice." He glanced around the foyer, which had been updated with gray hardwood floors, stylish furniture, and a coffee and tea station to greet guests. "It's hard to believe this is the same inn."

Tana stared at the screen, her pulse racing as she prepared to click the button that would publish the website—and re-open the inn for business. All the months of preparation, of worry, of sweat and tears, of doubts and fears—all of it led up to this moment. Even though Tana wasn't the owner of the Inn at Dolphin Bay, she had promised her uncle that she would help him rehabilitate the business he'd dedicated his life to. What if she failed?

"There's no way to remove the terrible reviews we've gotten over the past few years," she murmured, more to herself than Reed. Reviews were the lifeblood of the hotel industry, and the ones that had trickled in since the start of the inn's deterioration had been unflattering, to put it mildly. Even though she'd updated all the travel review websites to include details of the inn's renovation and remodeling, she didn't know if it would be enough.

"The Inn at Dolphin Bay is practically a Maine institution," Reed pointed out, crouching beside her and covering her hand with his own. "I've heard enough from the chatter around town to know that everyone is excited for the grand reopening. And don't forget—Henry has a new secret weapon."

"What's that?" Tana said with a frown.

Reed winked at her. "My mother. Edie Dawes is a social butterfly—she has the name of practically every woman in the state in her personal address book. She's already starting to spread the word among her friend groups, and several of them are planning to book stays in the coming months." He nudged her hand. "Go on; do it. You've worked hard, and now it's time for you and Henry to reap the rewards."

Tana's eyes lingered on the preview page of the inn's new website. She had to admit, it was beautiful, and if she stumbled across it while looking for a vacation destination, she wouldn't hesitate to book a room. "Okay, here goes nothing," she said, pressing the publish button and then immediately squeezing her eyes shut as she released a long exhale.

She felt Reed's hands on her own once more, and then he was tugging her to her feet and resting his hands on her waist. When she opened her eyes, she found herself staring into his pale blue ones. "I'm proud of you," he murmured, leaning forward to brush his lips gently over hers.

She let out a sigh and wrapped her arms around his neck, leaning her head against his chest and listening to the steady pounding of his heart. At times over the past few months, the amount of work needed to resurrect the inn from its state of disrepair had seemed overwhelming, but she had met every task with determination and the will to succeed. It had been exhausting, and only now, in this brief moment of respite, did she allow herself a moment to relax.

Then she caught sight of the clock hanging on the wall behind the inn's front desk and straightened up again. "I didn't realize how late it had gotten! The reporter is going to be here at any moment, and I haven't even made coffee yet." She glanced around the room desperately, as if hoping two mugs of coffee and a plate of refreshments would appear, and then turned to make a beeline for the kitchen.

"Whoa there." Reed grabbed her arm, his eyes dancing with amusement as he saw her frantic expression. "You take a minute and clear your head for the interview. I'll go make the coffee." He brushed past her and headed down the hallway, whistling under his breath.

Tana watched him walk away, a smile playing across her lips, and then she sank into the desk chair and ran a hand through her hair. The past few days had been madness as they scrambled to ready the inn for reopening, and what she wanted more than anything right now was to grab a chair, a picnic basket, and a good book, and head straight for the beach, losing herself in the sound of the waves crashing against the shore and the feel of the sand between her toes.

But after days of contacting every newspaper in Maine, she'd finally heard back from the travel reporter at the *Maine Herald*, the most-read daily newspaper in the state. As luck would have it, the woman used to vacation with her parents in Dolphin Bay when she was a child, and even though they hadn't stayed at the inn, she remembered it well... and had been more than willing to interview Tana on the grand reopening. It was a golden opportunity, and even though Tana was nervous about the prospect of being interviewed, she was determined to give the inn—and Uncle Henry—the publicity they deserved.

Tana slid her compact mirror out of her bag and refreshed her makeup, then ran a comb through her hair and straightened her blouse. As she was sliding her bag back under the desk, she heard the telltale sound of tires crunching on gravel, and glanced out the window to see a man pulling a rented golf cart into the inn's parking lot. A woman sat beside him, wearing a navy business suit and heels, and she picked her way across the lot as he grabbed some camera equipment and hurried to catch up with her.

"Hi, you must be Carrie," Tana said as she opened the door to greet the pair.

The woman stuck out her hand to shake Tana's,

her grip surprisingly strong. "Thanks for having us. This is a beautiful island—I haven't been here in years, and I've forgotten just how lovely it really is." She gestured toward the man, who was still standing in the parking lot, his camera aimed at the inn's exterior as he snapped photo after photo. "James is one of our photographers. He'll be taking some shots to accompany the article—both exterior and interior, if that's okay."

"That'll be just fine," Tana said happily, leading Carrie into the inn's parlor area and directing her toward the pale blue leather couch that she and Edie had picked out together. "I appreciate you coming out here, and for agreeing to write the article, of course." She glanced around the room, then out the inn's gorgeous picture window that stretched nearly floor to ceiling. "This is a special place, and I can't be more thrilled to reintroduce it to the public."

Reed came in just then, balancing a carafe of coffee and several mugs. He set them on the coffee table and strode out again, returning a few moments later with a tray of pastries and a handful of plates. He positioned them next to the coffee and turned to leave, but Tana stopped him with a soft hand on the arm. "Stay," she mouthed as Carrie slipped a notebook and tape recorder from her bag and placed them on the table. "Please."

He grinned at her and slid into the seat beside her, and she felt her whole body relaxing as his presence filled the room. This was a big moment for the inn, and for Uncle Henry, and having Reed by her side would definitely ease some of her nerves. Being around him always brought Tana a sense of calm, of peace… of pure happiness. He caught her eye, and the love she saw reflected in his gaze caused a lump of emotion to form in her throat.

"Before we begin," Carrie said, leaning forward to help herself to a mug of coffee, "I want to clarify that you are not the current owner of the inn, correct?"

"Yes." Tana filled her own mug and took a sip, shooting Reed a grateful look for his thoughtfulness. "Henry Turner, my great uncle, is the owner, but he's a little reserved and wasn't comfortable sitting down for an interview. I moved back to Dolphin Bay a few months ago to help him with the renovation and reopening. It's been a very hands-on process for me, and I'm able to answer any questions you might have."

"Great." Carrie clicked open her pen and flipped on the tape recorder. "I'd like to start with a little bit about the inn's history. It's my understanding that this building has been in your family for several generations. Who was the original owner, and when did he or she decide to begin operating it as an inn?"

"The original owners were Martha and Michael Turner, my uncle's great-grandparents," Tana said, settling back in her chair to begin recounting the familiar story. "They had three sons, and this was their family home. Two of the sons died in the Civil War, and the third came home with major injuries, including an amputated leg. Times were hard after the war, and money was tight, especially with the loss of their sons, and so Martha had the idea of converting her sons' former bedrooms into rooms for rent. She had close ties to the community on Dolphin Bay and the surrounding islands, and a keen business sense, because before long, she was booked year-round. Eventually, her son recovered from his injuries and took over the business, turning it into a full-fledged hotel operation. That was Henry's grandfather, who then passed it to his son, Henry's father. Stephen Turner died when Henry was a teenager, leaving him to run the inn ever since."

"That's quite a story," Carrie said appreciatively, jotting a few lines in her notebook before returning her attention to Tana. "If you don't mind, I'd love to have a look around the inn while we continue chatting." She grabbed the tape recorder and motioned to the photographer, who had appeared in the doorway and was looking around with interest, his camera slung around his neck.

"Of course, I'd be more than happy to show you around," Tana said, taking one last sip of her coffee before rising to her feet and beckoning for the others to join her. For the next hour, she gave Carrie and James the grand tour of the inn while discussing its history, the significance it had to the community, and the renovations it had undergone over the past few months. While she spoke, Tana felt a sense of pride at all they had accomplished since the start of the summer. It had truly taken a village, and Reed, Edie, Daphne, and Luke and his crew were just that.

"One last question," Carrie said as Tana led the way into the parlor and the group settled back onto the couches. She helped herself to a pastry, brushing crumbs from her lips as she rifled through the bag at her feet. "Here we go," she said, pulling out a magazine and dropping it onto the table beside the carafe. When Tana saw the cover, her heart stuttered to a halt, and from somewhere beside her, she could hear Reed's snort of annoyance.

It was the most current issue of a tabloid magazine, and half the front cover was dedicated to Derek and Lucia, both wearing sunglasses and holding hands as they frolicked on some Southern California beach. She was wearing a barely-there yellow bikini, her olive skin smooth and perfect, her long hair hanging almost to her tiny waist. He was bare-chested and tan, his silver hair gleaming in the sunshine.

Tana felt sick.

Carrie gave her a small smile. "I usually don't delve into my interviewee's personal lives, but I think your story will add even more interest to the inn. You said you came here a few months ago to help out your uncle—does that also coincide with your husband's affair with actress Lucia Mondelo?"

Tana felt Reed tense beside her as her cheeks flamed with embarrassment. Carrie's face turned sympathetic. "And I'm assuming you know they recently announced their engagement? They gave a joint interview for a story in *People* this week."

"I did know," Tana ground out, teeth clenched. She could feel Reed's questioning gaze on her; she still hadn't mentioned the news of Derek's engage-ment to him. She gave Carrie a hard look. "I'm having a hard time understanding how my personal life is in any way related to the reopening of an inn that's been around for more than a century."

The reporter shrugged. "Human interest. The better the story, the more eyeballs on the article, the more likely you'll get business. It's a win all around."

"Except for Tana." Reed's hand was on her arm, but she barely felt it. "I think this is a good time to wrap up the interview." He made to stand up, but Tana stopped him with a firm head shake.

"No, it's—" She took a deep breath. "It's okay. I don't appreciate the intrusion into my private life, but that's not really your fault. It's Derek's." She eyed the reporter, whose tape recorder was at the ready; behind her, the cameraman was surreptitiously snapping photos, earning an angry glare from Reed. "It's public knowledge that my husband had an affair with Lucia, yes. We were married for more than twenty years, and to say I was devastated would be a terrible understatement."

She straightened her shoulders. "But I'm not the only woman who has gone through heartbreak, and to any of your readers who are dealing with betrayal or a broken marriage, know this." Tana stared straight at the camera, as though she were speaking directly to them. "You can and will come out of this the other side. And"—she reached for Reed's hand, feeling the reassuring pressure of his presence—"it will be better than you ever imagined."

Reed's smile was gentle as she caught his eye, and they gazed at each other for a long moment as the rest of the world fell away. The *click-click* of James's camera shattered the silence, and Tana blinked, pulling herself back to the task at hand. Carrie was nodding, chewing on her bottom lip as she scribbled line after line into her notebook before finally snapping it closed and grinning at Tana.

"That's great, Tana, thanks. I'm sure our readers are going to appreciate it. And thank you again for the tour of the inn—it's a beautiful place, and I'm so happy to hear that it has overcome its recent troubles. I'm planning to run a front-page feature in the paper's travel section this weekend, so you should get plenty of eyes on it and hopefully"—she crossed her fingers and winked—"plenty of bookings. I can assure you, I'll be back myself, with kids and husband in tow. I could use a vacation."

"Couldn't we all," Tana murmured as the reporters packed up their belongings. A few minutes later, she was waving them out the door, watching as they traipsed to their golf cart, dumped their gear inside, and slid into their seats. She stayed in the doorway until they were out of sight, the rumble of their engine a distant noise against the crashing of the sea.

When she turned back to Reed, his arms were open, beckoning, and she practically fell into them. "Have I ever told you how amazing you are?" he murmured into her hair as he stroked his fingers up and down her spine, eliciting a shiver. "If someone asked me those questions, I'd be furious. But you— you handled them with grace and poise." He quieted for a moment, his hands now tangled in her hair. Then he asked, "Why didn't you tell me? About the engagement."

"I'm not sure," she admitted, pulling back to look into his face, so beloved. "I haven't wanted to talk about it, I guess." She sighed heavily. "Jax thinks I need closure. He wants me to confront Derek, get everything from the past few months off my chest. Which is a horrible idea," she added with a laugh, then frowned when she saw Reed's mouth pursed in thought. "Oh no, not you too."

"It's not the worst idea I've ever heard," he said, still looking thoughtful. Then he shrugged. "But that's your business—if you want to speak to Derek, I'll support you. If you don't, I'll support that too." Then he grinned at her, his eyes crinkling at the corners in the way she loved so much. "By the way, did you mean what you said to the reporter? About things being better than you could have imagined?"

"More than you could ever know," Tana said softly, slipping her hand into his and standing shoulder to shoulder with him as they gazed out at the rolling sea.

CHAPTER 9

*L*ydia lay back on the sand, striped beach towel spread beneath her, and gazed up at the sparkling sky. It was the kind of perfect summer day she always dreamed about when she was up to her eyeballs in Maine's snowy winters— even the smell of hot dogs was on the air, courtesy of a local vendor who had set up shop on the edge of the sand. Crowded around him were beachgoers of every age, young and old and everywhere in between, holding paper plates with hot dogs loaded with ketchup and mustard, napkins fluttering in the wind. A girl around the age of six was sipping from a paper cup of soda, chasing the floating straw around with her lips, her salty hair tangled in the sea breeze, shoulders dappled with freckles. Lydia smiled when she caught her eye, feeling the familiar pang of what might have been—what *should* have been—and then letting it go in a soft exhale before turning toward the sea.

An angry voice reached her ear, out of place amid the laughing vacationers and squawking seagulls, and she turned to see a man with dark hair sitting in the sand a short distance away, talking furiously into his phone, one hand waving around his head as he spoke. Lydia squinted, and after a moment of trying to place him, realized that it was Jared, Maura's soon-to-be husband. She watched from the corner of her eye as he yanked the phone away from his ear, jamming his finger against the screen to end the call before tossing it to the side, where it landed face up in the sand. Then he dropped his head and raked his fingers through his hair, making it stand on end.

After a moment's hesitation, Lydia stood and picked her way across the sand toward him, avoiding a boy and girl building an elaborate sand castle far too close to the water's edge to keep it safe. When Jared saw her approaching, he squared his shoulders and raised a hand in greeting.

"Everything okay?" she asked, hovering over him, unsure whether she should even be there. But duty called; the groom was her client, for better or worse, and she needed to make sure there wasn't a brewing crisis that she needed to stop in its tracks.

He stared out at the water for a long moment, his eyes tracking the movement of a seagull as it dipped in and out of the waves, before turning to her, raising a hand to shield his face from the sun's glare. "I don't know," he said, and he sounded so morose that Lydia sank onto the sand beside him, tugging her knees up to her chest and wrapping her arms around them as the breeze blew her hair around her face.

"Want to talk about it?" she asked, brushing a strand of hair from her mouth. The sun was hitting the water directly now, casting golden rays across the rippling surface; this, she decided, was paradise.

Jared grabbed a stick that had washed to shore and began tracing a line in the sand, his forehead scrunched in concentration. Lydia watched him for a while, digging her toes deeper into the sand, scooping it into her fingers and letting it pass through like a waterfall. "I didn't come from money, you know," he finally murmured, eyes still on the stick. He raised his gaze to hers. "I had a single mother who worked two jobs to keep the lights on and food on the table."

Lydia made a soft sound, unsure what to say—

and where he was going with this. He sighed loudly and tossed the stick as far as he could into the waves, watching as it skimmed off the water's surface before sinking into the depths. "When I met Maura, I had no idea about any of this. What her father did, how she grew up, nothing. She was just a girl with the most gorgeous smile I'd ever seen, and a zest for life that was infectious. I couldn't wait to marry her." He laughed, but the sound held no humor. "That's when the trouble started. The ring."

He gave Lydia a bitter smile. "I thought I'd picked out the perfect one—a sapphire, to match the blue in her eyes, surrounded by a cluster of diamonds. It wasn't the most expensive one in the shop, but I thought it was perfect. When I got down on one knee and opened the box, I saw the disappointment in her eyes. She said yes, and the next day, her father asked me to return it and find a better one. He said his daughter deserved diamonds. Can you believe that?"

He snorted, then shook his head. "It all went downhill from there. As soon as we started planning the wedding—as soon as *she* started planning the wedding, I should say, because she hasn't involved me at all—it's like... it's like she turned into a different person." He combed his fingers through the sand as he spoke, his eyes on the horizon. "I'm not even sure I want to marry her anymore. The girl I fell in love with… I can barely even see her."

He speared Lydia with a look, his lips twisted into a wry smile. "I don't even know why I'm telling you all this. I know it's not part of your job description."

"Oh, you have no idea how many things fall under my job description," Lydia said, plucking a seashell from the sand and turning it over in her fingers. It was smooth as butter, pink with lines of gray running from top to bottom.

"When I decided to become a wedding planner, I thought it would be all about throwing the most perfect party of each client's life. Since then, I've come to realize that the wedding itself is almost like an afterthought. So much goes into planning the darn thing that barely any of my brides and grooms enjoy their actual day—they're too stressed, and exhausted, and worried that everything isn't going to be perfect. And it usually isn't, because that's life."

She shrugged. "But that doesn't mean it isn't perfect anyway. If that makes sense."

"It does." Jared nodded. "It absolutely does." He began flattening the sand around him with the palm of his hand, slowly, methodically, while Lydia watched without really seeing. "What now?" he asked into the silence that stretched between them. He gave her a desperate look. "Tomorrow's the rehearsal. And after that… Do I really want to marry into this family?" He wasn't asking Lydia the question; he was asking himself.

"Only you can answer that," Lydia said. "But I will say, it's normal for people to have doubts before a wedding. It's a big step, one that isn't easy to undo." She thought back to her own wedding day, the excitement, the anticipation, the feeling of joy knowing that her whole life was laid out before her, just the way she'd always dreamed of. Never a doubt, never a moment of uncertainty had entered her mind.

Look what good that had done her.

"Are you married?" Jared asked, then immediately shook his head, looking chagrinned. "I'm sorry. I'm being intrusive. Please don't feel like you have to answer that."

"No, it's okay." Lydia brushed another strand of hair from her mouth, her lips sticky from the salt-stained air. She drew her arms tighter around herself, her eyes on the ferry making its way into the harbor, the faces of the occupants barely visible at this distance. "I was married, but I'm not anymore."

She laughed. "So don't take my advice as gospel. It isn't. I spend my days and nights planning other people's weddings when I couldn't make my own relationship work. How's that for irony?" She didn't know why she was being so candid with him, but once the words started flowing, they were hard to stop.

"What happened?" Jared was watching her out of the corner of his eye, his hand still trailing in the sand. "Did he change?"

"No." In Lydia's mind, the years melted away as she pictured Luke's face, so beloved. The boyish smile, the eyes that always danced with laughter. He was her golden boy, through and through. She cupped her face in both hands, blinking back the memories—and the tears.

"We were high school sweethearts who got married right out of college. Everything was great between us until we tried to start a family." Her voice caught, but she forged on, aware of Jared's full attention on her.

"I, we, were unable to have children. There were many moments of hope, but they always ended in heartbreak. He wanted to stop trying; I didn't, not really. I would have gone to the ends of the earth to have a baby, but he didn't want us to live in misery anymore."

She lifted one shoulder in a shrug. "No one was wrong. No one was right. We just couldn't reach each other through our grief. Eventually, I couldn't take it anymore. I left. Walked out the door one morning when he left for work and never came home. I broke his heart. Mine, too."

She toed at the sand, caught the edge of her foot on a piece of sea glass. A pinprick of blood bloomed on her skin, and she stretched out her foot to let the ocean water carry it away.

Jared was quiet for a time after that, his shoulders hunched, his body wilting in on itself. "But before then?" he asked, his voice so quiet it was almost carried away on the sea breeze. "You were happy."

"The happiest." The words came out broken. "We were the happiest."

She cleared her throat and looked at him. "No one can tell you what to do. Only you know what's best for you, what's in your heart. But if you love her, you might be able to find a way to overcome your differences. I wish I had. Now look at me." She gestured to herself, giving Jared a self-deprecating smile. "Middle-aged, alone. It's harder to find love now. I probably never will again."

"Oh, I don't know about that." Jared raised his eyebrows and tilted his head slightly to the left. "This whole time we've been talking, that guy over there's barely been able to keep his eyes off you."

Lydia frowned, following his gaze down the sand.

And found herself looking directly into Luke's eyes.

THE WIND WAS WHIPPING up around him, the day growing cooler as it melted into evening, but Luke didn't care. He was too busy focused on her… and the man sitting beside her, huddled too close, his posture just a little too casual.

She had someone. Why didn't she mention she had someone? Somewhere in that thirty-second phone call they'd had a couple months ago, when she'd warned him she was returning to the island, couldn't she have found an extra moment or two to slip *that* into the conversation?

Luke, it's me. Lydia. I just wanted you to know, in case we run into each other, that I have a wedding in Dolphin Bay in a few weeks. And oh, yeah, I'll be bringing my boyfriend. My much younger boyfriend. So if you see us around town, don't rip off his head and hurl it into the ocean.

Okay, that last part was an improvisation, Luke thought as he tried to focus his attention elsewhere. Further up the beach, a man was selling hot dogs, and while the smell of charcoal and an open grill would normally have him digging for his wallet, today it was making him sick.

His eyes wandered along the sand in the opposite direction, toward a group of twenty-somethings playing volleyball in the surf. The women were gorgeous, with long legs and tan skin, their hair highlighted in the sun's rays as it flew around their shoulders while they dove and ran, arms outstretched, bikinis testing the limits of gravity.

But they couldn't hold a candle to her.

Like a magnet, his attention was drawn back to her—to *them*—only this time, he realized, the wind knocked from his lungs... she was looking right back at him.

The man said something to her, and she got to her feet, sliding her sandals back on and walking toward him, kicking up sand as she approached. Luke watched her, frozen, his heart pounding in his ears. She looked the same as she did on that day five years ago, when she'd walked out of his life forever.

No. Not forever.

"Luke." Her voice was wary, her face tight. "Hello." There was a stiffness about her, a protectiveness in the way she hugged her arms around herself, as if to ward him off. He felt his heart sinking a little, and his hands clenched automatically at his sides.

Lydia was looking at him now, her expression softening a fraction. "It's good to see you." She reached out a hand, as if they were mere acquaintances seeing each other after many years. "How have you been? What a surprise running into you here."

She glanced back toward the man she was with, who was now gazing out at the sea, his muscular shoulders hunched. Luke felt his anger flare; the man, whoever he was, wasn't even watching them, wasn't even concerned that Lydia was talking to him.

"It's not a surprise." Luke got to his feet, squaring off against her. He could see the surprise in her eyes —and something else, too. A flicker of apprehension. Of regret? "I came here on purpose, hoping I'd find you." He waved his hand in a circle, encompassing the beach. "This is your favorite spot. Did you think I'd forgotten?"

It was something more, too. The place where

they'd gotten engaged, one windswept October night when the stars were scattered across the sky like diamonds and reflected in her eyes as he held her tight and swayed in time to the music only they could hear.

The sorrow was evident in her gaze this time— fleeting, a momentary lowering of the barrier between them, but he caught it all the same. When he tried to find it again, it was gone, replaced by a blank look that he knew had been carefully constructed, designed to keep him out.

"Why?" she asked, her hand going to her hair as it billowed around her in the breeze. She smoothed it down, her forehead furrowing. "Why did you come here to find me, I mean."

Luke inhaled sharply and met her eyes. "To tell you that I'm still in love with you."

CHAPTER 10

"*D*aphne, we need to talk."

Daphne had barely registered the sound of the door opening, and glanced up from her spot behind the counter to see Tana standing in the bakery's doorway, arms folded across her chest, expression pained. She set down her pen and pushed away the calculator she'd been using to tally up her projected first month's expenses, then looked at her friend with raised eyebrows.

"Why so serious? Don't tell me you're breaking up with me."

She expected a smile, a snicker, a reaction of some kind, but if anything, Tana only looked more pained. "May I?" She stepped into the bakery and lowered herself into the nearest chair while a concerned Daphne came around the counter and joined her at the small table.

"What's wrong?" she asked, leaning forward to rest her hand on Tana's arm. "Did something happen at the inn? Did the interview go poorly?" Earlier that day, Tana had been interviewed by a popular newspaper about the inn's grand reopening, and Daphne knew her friend was nervous.

"No, that was fine," Tana said with a wave of her hand. Then she winced. "Other than the reporter blindsiding me with a question about Derek and Lucia's engagement, of course, but that's not why I'm here."

"Ouch." Daphne leaned back and folded her arms across her chest. Outside the bakery's window, a mother and her two children strolled by, looking inside with interest. Daphne gave them a smile and a wave, then turned her attention back to her friend. "So what's up?"

Tana chewed on her bottom lip for a moment, stalling for time. Then she heaved a sigh and said, "It's about Luke."

"Luke?" Daphne sat forward. "What about him? Is he okay?"

"He's fine, he's fine." Another wave of the hand, and Daphne could tell that Tana's nerves were kicking up a notch. What in the world was going on?

"It's just…" Tana winced. "I don't think you should date him. And please, before you get mad," she added hastily, "I'm not trying to barge in on your love life. Normally I would mind my own business, but…" She let her voice trail off, and Daphne filled the silence with a laugh and a knowing smile.

"I think what you're trying to say is that you don't want me falling for a guy who's already in love with someone else?"

Tana looked surprised, then nodded. "That about sums it up, yeah." She raised her eyebrows at Daphne. "You already knew?"

"Do pigs like mud?" Daphne snorted. "Of course I know. I tried to ignore it at first—I mean, it's been an open secret for years that he's still carrying a torch for Lydia, and I figured he'd eventually get over it. He seemed into me, and I don't think that was an act."

She toyed with the hem of her shirt, eyes downcast, heart a little heavier than it had been a moment ago. "But if I really think hard about it, I can recognize that the closer we got to her arrival on the island, the more distant he got." She shrugged. "It's okay. Our relationship just wasn't meant to take that form. We'll still be friends, though. He's a good guy, and he can't help who he loves."

Jax's face flashed across her mind, but she quickly banished it.

Tana was studying her carefully. "Are you okay?"

"I'm fine. Honestly, I haven't had time to give it that much thought." Daphne waved her arm around to indicate the bakery. "Things have been so hectic getting ready for the opening that I haven't had time to dwell on it. But if you're asking"—she hesitated, considering Tana's question—"then I guess I'm a little disappointed, yes. I got my hopes up, thought maybe someone was out there for me after all."

She rubbed her forehead, which was suddenly throbbing. "I don't want to be alone. But it's starting to look like I'll end up that way."

"First of all," Tana said, her voice turning stern, "you're not alone, and you never will be. And second of all." She stopped speaking abruptly, then shook her head and said, "No, I'm going to say it." Her determined eyes found Daphne's. "I don't think Luke is the only one who's still in love with someone else."

Jax's face again, quick as a flash. *Stop it*, Daphne warned herself.

"I have no idea what you're talking about," she said to Tana.

"You do. And please"—Tana leaned forward, clutching the edge of the table—"do something about it before it's too late."

"Uncle Jax? Do you have a minute?"

Jax lowered the book he was reading and glanced up to find Emery staring down at him, shifting uncertainly from foot to foot. He had been sitting on the inn's wraparound porch, enjoying a few minutes of relaxation as the sun spread its last rays across the coral-streaked sky.

"Sure," he said, bookmarking his page and patting the chair next to him. Things had been so hectic over the past few days that he hadn't spent much time with his only niece; besides, he didn't want to take any quality time away from Tana.

"What's up?" He glanced over at her face, frowning when he noticed that her eyes were red-rimmed and puffy, as if she'd been recently crying. He sat up straighter and leaned toward her, concerned. "Are you okay?"

"No, I'm not." She withdrew a tissue from her pocket and dabbed at her eyes, then blew her nose, shaking her head as she stared out over the horizon.

"Everything's a mess lately, and I don't know what to do." She inhaled a shaky breath, then let it out on a soft sigh.

"Talk to me," Jax said gently, angling his chair so that he was facing her. "Tell me what's going on."

"You mean other than the fact that the last few months have been the worst of my life?" Emery laughed bitterly as she flung her long hair over her shoulders. Then she speared him with a look. "Imagine your family falling apart in the public eye —your father deciding to flaunt an affair with a woman almost as young as you, the tabloids soaking up every last juicy detail of it."

Tears filled her eyes again, and she swiped them away with the back of one hand. "It's been humiliating. All of my friends have been talking about it; some making jokes, even purposely cutting out pictures of the two of them from those awful magazines and leaving them around my apartment for me to find. It's sick. They don't get that this is my family, my life. They think that because I'm not a kid anymore, this hasn't been devastating. They're wrong."

As she spoke, Jax nodded along, his eyes warm with sympathy. He, too, was well aware of the chaos an unstable home life could cause, having been forced to deal with the demons that arose when his mother chose to practically abandon him and Tana in favor of traveling the world for work.

"Have you spoken to your mother about this?" he asked, then fell silent as Emery shook her head so vigorously her hair slapped against her cheeks.

"No way. Mom has enough going on; she doesn't need to worry about me, too. Besides, I'll be okay. I'll…" Her voice drifted off, but Jax could tell she was holding back. He waited patiently, not wanting to push her, sensing that she needed time to gather her thoughts.

Finally, she sighed again and said, "I'm not really on summer break right now. I…" She swallowed hard. "I've been so distracted that I've let things slip at school. I wasn't always going to my internship— there were some days when I could barely get out of bed, much less get myself together and put on a brave face. I'd gotten a once-in-a-lifetime opportunity, and I let it slip away. They fired me a few weeks ago. And my classes—"

She inhaled sharply. "I failed the semester. The dean put me on academic probation, which meant I had a chance to turn things around. But instead of doing that, I… I dropped out. I couldn't take it anymore. The pressure… the humiliation… any of it." Her head dropped into her hands, her hair cascading over her face like rain. She added, face still buried in her hands, "I don't know what possessed me to do it. One minute, I was doing what I loved, and the next…" She shook her head. "I was walking out the door."

Jax rested a comforting hand on Emery's arm as his niece dissolved into tears, her shoulders trembling. "What am I going to do?" she asked, her voice muffled by tears. "What's my mother going to say?"

"Well, I can't answer the first question, other than to say you'll figure it out, in time. But I can definitely answer the second one." Jax's voice was confident, and Emery tipped her head up, meeting his gaze with puffy eyes. "Your mother is going to say that she loves you, and she's proud of you, and she'll do whatever it takes to make sure you're happy again."

He gripped her arm. "Don't give up, and don't let yourself fall victim to an endless loop of what-ifs. Look no further than me. Look what's happened in my life—I lost the restaurant, my livelihood, sometimes my whole reason for getting up in the morning. I thought I was done for, a has-been. But you never know when new opportunities are waiting around the corner."

"Like Daphne?" Emery gave him a sly smile through her tears.

Jax recoiled, removing his hand from her arm. "What?"

"Oh, come on, Uncle Jax." She straightened the tissue in her hand and patted her eyes again. "I see the way you two look at each other—the whole world does."

Jax opened his mouth, then closed it again with a shake of his head. "I don't know about all that, but I do know that what I'm telling you is true. You will figure this out, and you will come out of it the other side." He gave her a soft smile. "But there's no reason to do it alone, and there's no shame in asking for help. The future is unexpected, and uncertain, and at times, it's downright terrifying, and that's okay— that's a lesson I'm learning every day."

She was quiet for several long moments as they listened to the seagulls crying overhead and the waves lapping against the shore. In the distance, Jax saw a kite in the shape of a butterfly soaring along the beach, its wings fluttering wildly whenever they caught the breeze. He couldn't see them, but he could imagine the children running after it, whooping and laughing as it careened into the twilight sky.

Finally, she turned to him and whispered, "Thank you," her brown eyes glittering in the waning light. She stood, then leaned over to kiss him lightly on the cheek before padding off, disappearing inside the inn, leaving the door to swing shut behind her with a soft *click*.

Jax rested his hand on the book he'd been reading, not yet ready to return to its pages. He thought of everything he'd just told his niece, every bit of wisdom he'd tried to impart. He hoped it would make a difference. She was lost right now, and that was okay—everyone was a little lost sometimes. In the end, all that mattered was how you managed to pick yourself up, dust yourself off, and keep your head held high as you tried to navigate the twisting, winding path of life.

It was the same advice he gave himself on a daily basis, a mantra he repeated when the doubts threatened to overwhelm him. In time, he would see whether it worked.

He glanced at the sky, deciding to make good use of what little light remained, and slid his bookmark out from between the pages and continued reading. He hadn't gotten far when his phone rang, shattering the silence and startling him. Retrieving it from his pocket, he glanced at the caller ID and noted the Florida area code.

"Jax Keller," he answered, setting his book to the side once more, this time with more than a little regret.

"Hey, Jax, Steve Neuman here. How are you doing?" The restaurant investor spoke in his usual booming voice, but Jax could tell from the pace of his words that he was in a hurry. Without bothering to wait for Jax to respond, Steve pressed on, "I have an issue, and I'm hoping you can help me."

"Sure," Jax said with a frown, balancing the phone on one shoulder as he lifted a glass of lemonade to his lips. He took a long sip, then set it back down, realizing that his stomach was starting to form knots. He'd been spending long hours over the past few days planning out his menu to present to the investor, and he hoped Steve wasn't backing out. Had he already found the chef for his new bistro?

And why did that thought bring Jax some small measure of relief?

"Something came up and I won't be able to travel to Dolphin Bay on our original date." Jax could hear Steve clacking away on his keyboard in the background. "Can we move it up a few weeks? I'll be in your area this weekend, and I can make it out to the island on Monday evening."

Monday evening? Jax shot up in his chair. As in three days from now?

"Well, I—"

"It's the only day that will work," Steve said. "Sorry to throw off your schedule like this, but I'd still love to meet you—but if it doesn't happen on Monday, it doesn't happen at all."

Jax's eyebrows shot into his hairline at the man's curt tone, but he tempered any of his own annoyance as he said, "Okay, I can make that work. I'll shoot you the inn's address via email, and I'll see you then."

"Great. Thanks." Steve sounded relieved. "Looking forward to it."

Click.

Jax stared at the phone, its screen now black.

What had he just agreed to?

CHAPTER 11

"This will be your moment, so try to relax and enjoy it as best you can," Lydia said, clipboard in hand as she stood beside the aisle where Maura clung to her father's arm. Jared stood where the canopy would be, his hands folded in front of him, his expression uneasy. She gave him a reassuring smile, which he returned, his face lighting up for the briefest of moments before his eyes landed on Maura once more and he shifted uncomfortably on his feet.

Lydia had orchestrated countless wedding rehearsals. This one had to take the cake.

The groom looked like he was being marched to his own beheading. The bride was in a rage because her husband-to-be had flat-out refused to take the helicopter back to the mainland to exchange his tie for one whose specific shade of blue matched her expectations—which explained his presence on the beach yesterday.

The mother of the bride clearly had overindulged in her drink of choice, and was swaying from side to side like a seasick sailor, every so often grabbing Lydia's arm for support. The father of the bride was barking orders to anyone who would listen—mostly Lydia, although a few unsuspecting seagulls had gotten in his way as well, one depositing a gift Lydia couldn't have chosen better herself squarely onto his shiny black shoes.

The groom's mother and brother were standing off to the side, taking in the entire spectacle with identical bemused expressions, the mother every so often shooting her son a worried glance, though he refused to meet her eyes.

And in the middle of it all was Lydia, who had her own problems to deal with, thank you very much.

I'm still in love with you.

Seven words, rattling around in her brain, making concentrating on the task at hand nothing short of impossible. The look in his eyes when he'd said them—earnest, sincere... hopeful. She couldn't get it out of her head.

Nor could she forgive herself for her reaction.

"Stop." She held up her hand. "Please, don't say that to me." Her voice was pleading.

Luke shook his head, determined, the glint of hope still present in his gaze. "I have to, Lydia. You feel the same way—I know you do. How could you not, after everything we were to each other?" He reached out his hand for hers, but she batted it away.

"You're wrong, Luke. I'm... I'm sorry."

And then she'd turned from him, walking away without a backward glance or even a goodbye.

Thinking about it now made her feel sick.

She'd panicked—and could she really blame herself for that? Seeing him again brought everything they'd been through slamming back into her like a freight train. The monthly prayers. The sleepless nights. The hope, the glimmer of light, and then the soul-crushing devastation. How could she look him in the eyes again and not see the destruction of all they'd dreamed of, all they'd planned for? It was why she had run from that life in the first place.

And why she was still running.

The father of the bride coughed impatiently, drawing Lydia back to the present moment, and she offered Maura a wide smile and said, "Okay, are you ready to practice the walk of your life? On the count of three…"

She pressed her clipboard to her chest as she watched Maura and her father take careful steps down the aisle, arm in arm, him looking proud, her looking self-conscious. Her free hand fluttered to her hair, and then her dress, before she settled it in front of her, carrying an imaginary bouquet of flowers. Jared's face softened as she walked toward him, and for a moment, as she watched the two of them silently communicating with each other, Lydia could see through their eyes the rest of the world dropping away.

Or maybe it was just her imagination, a ghost of the past she'd never truly let go of.

For the next twenty minutes, she walked them through the ceremony, noting how their faces simultaneously tightened as they turned toward each other to deliver their practice vows. Maura spoke in a robotic voice, as if she'd been rehearsing in front of a mirror, and Jared kept fumbling the lines and glancing at the notes he'd scribbled on a scrap of paper. Lydia tried to keep from cringing as they turned and smiled at their parents, who were clapping in a feeble sort of way, the bride's mother raising a flask she'd unearthed from somewhere and taking a celebratory swig before pinching a passing venue staff member on the bottom.

All in all, Lydia couldn't wait to get away, and after ensuring that everything was in order for the rehearsal dinner, which was to be held right on the sand, beneath tents of white adorned with shimmering fairy lights, she managed to slip away, letting a soft sigh of relief escape as she slipped behind the wheel of her golf cart. Tomorrow couldn't be over soon enough.

And neither, she thought, could tonight—because she knew the hours that stretched ahead would be endless, her mind caught in a vicious cycle of what-ifs, Luke's face haunting her as the minutes ticked on and the island sky darkened to a black so thick you could get lost in it.

Good thing for her she was already lost.

"Henry? This is a surprise. Please, come in."

Reed Dawes stepped back and opened his door further, beckoning the older man inside. He cleared a couple of takeout cartons from his coffee table and tossed a few pieces of clothing scattered on the couch into his bedroom, then gestured for Henry to sit down.

Once he was settled into an armchair, his cane by his side, Reed headed into the kitchen and grabbed two bottles of soda from the fridge. Tana was out to dinner on the mainland with her daughter, and in her absence, he had quickly reverted to his bachelor ways—dinner in the living room, feet up on the couch, television remote in one hand and ice-cold can of beer in the other.

He'd expected to fall asleep to the sounds of ESPN blaring from the speakers. He hadn't planned on a visitor, especially Henry Turner.

The old man didn't make social calls. In fact, Reed wasn't entirely sure if Henry even knew what a social call *was*. Reed's mother must have been rubbing off on him after all.

He returned to the living room and handed Henry a soda, then sank into a chair opposite him. "What brings you here tonight? Did you need some help at the inn?" For the past few years, long before Tana's arrival on the island, Reed had served as the inn's volunteer handyman, though thanks to Henry's unwillingness to accept help and overall stubborn nature, he'd had to do most of it on the sly.

"No, nothing like that." Henry was cradling the

drink in his left hand, which, along with his left leg, had suffered a partial loss of mobility due to a recent stroke. He had been making positive strides in physical therapy, though, and Edie liked to joke that before long, he would be tangoing on the beach with her under the stars.

Which, frankly, was an image Reed could have done without.

"Everything okay?" he asked, frowning as he noted the strained expression on Henry's face.

"Yes, erm—" Henry cleared his throat, then took a long sip of his drink before setting it down on the arm of his chair, carefully avoiding Reed's gaze. "I have a request for you. An important one."

"Okay, shoot." Reed relaxed into his seat, then took a swig of his own soda. He'd already muted the television when he heard the knock on the door, but he reached for the remote and switched it off completely, watching as the screen went black before returning his attention to Henry. "What can I do for you?"

Henry looked straight at him then, his faded green eyes steely with determination. "I'd like your blessing." He inhaled sharply. "To marry your mother."

Then, before Reed could formulate a response, he

held up a weathered hand. "I know, Edie's an inde-
pendent woman, and she'd probably shake her finger
right in my face if she knew that I was here. But as
for me, I'm an old-fashioned man, and this… well,
it's important to me. I've only got one chance at this,
and I want to get it right from the start."

Reed noticed the man's hands were trembling,
and he quickly averted his eyes—the last thing he
wanted to do was inadvertently call attention to the
fact that Henry was nervous.

Instead, Reed blew out a long breath, ending
with, "Wow, Henry, I don't know what to say. You're
right about one thing, though"—his eyes crinkled in
a smile—"my mother would give you a good talking
to for coming here. Did you know my father didn't
even ask my grandfather for his blessing before he
proposed to her? And that was decades ago."

He shrugged. "As for me, I'm an old-fashioned
kind of guy, too, and I think it's nice." He leaned
forward, bracing his hands on his knees as he looked
directly into Henry's eyes. "I would be honored to
have you as part of the family, Mr. Turner."

A few months ago, Reed never would have imagined himself saying those words to anyone, especially Henry Turner. To think that his vibrant, lively
mother would fall for such a quiet, reserved man

would have never occurred to Reed in the past, but he'd also spent many years ignoring the subtle signs of their blossoming romance. Henry was a good man, and he made his mother happy. In the end, nothing mattered more than that.

Henry was silent for a long moment after that, his eyes on his hands, which were fidgeting in his lap. Finally, he looked up—and Reed was startled to see tears in the corners of the old man's eyes.

"Thank you for that," he whispered, then reached for his cane. "I won't take up any more of your time." He nodded toward the TV and takeout cartons with a knowing smile. "Pretty soon, I think you, too, are going to find yourself removed from the bachelor life. And when that happens"—he limped forward and stood over Reed—"for what it's worth, you have my blessing too."

The men shared a look of understanding, an acknowledgement that their lives had both changed for the better, thanks to the women who had stolen their hearts. When Henry turned to leave, Reed called after him, "So are you going to ask her now?"

"Oh no." Henry gave him a wistful smile as he stopped, hand on the doorknob. "There's someone else I have to speak with first."

And he was out the door before Reed could think

to ask him who. He sat on his couch for a few moments, listening to the thump-thump-thump of the old man's cane on the sidewalk outside, before he reached for the television remote once more. Flipping it on, he was just debating whether to tune in to the Red Sox game or try to find a movie that would keep him reasonably entertained until Tana stopped over later that evening when his phone lit up with a text message.

As he reached for it, Reed saw that the message was from Luke.

Had a rough day. Can I stop by? I'm a couple minutes away.

Reed typed in a quick *sure thing*, then spooned the last of his lo mein into his mouth, polished off an egg roll, and carried the takeout cartons into the kitchen. He eyed the fridge, then yanked it open and grabbed two bottles of beer—something told him Luke was going to need one, especially if Reed's hunch about Luke's rough day turned out to be true.

And he didn't see how it wouldn't. There could only be one reason for it.

He popped off the caps and was just carrying the bottles into his living room when he heard the knock at the door. Setting them down on the coffee table, he turned and opened it, finding himself face to face with an uncharacteristically disheveled Luke. His clothes were rumpled, as if he'd slept in them, and his hair was sticking up in several directions. A five-o'clock shadow had formed on his jawline, and the pronounced dark circles under his eyes told Reed that his friend hadn't gotten a wink of sleep last night, maybe even the night before too.

Wordlessly, he opened the door wider and ushered Luke inside. His friend collapsed onto the couch, immediately reaching for one of the beers, which he swallowed in three long gulps while Reed looked on, one eyebrow raised. He closed the door quietly and perched on the armchair opposite Luke, studying his strangely blank expression.

"Tell me," he said.

Luke laughed, though there wasn't a trace of happiness in his dull gaze. "What's there to tell? I laid it all out on the line, told her how I felt, and she shot me down." He stared down at his hands, which he was clenching and unclenching into fists in his lap. "I shouldn't have said anything to her at all. What's the point? Not only that," he added with a shake of his head, "but anything that might have been going on between me and Daphne is now dead in the water."

He gave Reed a wry smile. "Something tells me

she isn't going to want another date with a guy who just professed his undying love for another woman."

"True," Reed said, "but if I were you, I wouldn't worry too much about Daphne right now. You've only just started leaving friend territory, and I don't know if she's—"

He stopped, pursing his lips, and then reached for his own beer to cover the awkward moment. He had been about to point out that he wasn't sure if Daphne's heart was in the quasi-relationship either, given the expression of longing he'd seen on her face on more than one occasion when they were in Jax's presence, but why kick Luke while he was already down? Besides, he wasn't positive about what he'd seen, and hadn't even broached the subject with Tana.

"She was with another guy," Luke continued, as though he hadn't even heard what Reed had said. "Can you believe that?" His tone was rapidly changing from morose to angry. "She shows up here after five years and can't even do the decent thing of leaving her boyfriend or fiancé or husband or whatever he is at home." He eyed Reed's mostly full bottle of beer, then leaned forward and dropped his head to his hands.

"You don't know who he was," Reed offered,

trying without much success to look at the bright side of things. "He could have been a friend, or a coworker, or hey! Maybe he was a member of the wedding party, the groom or the best man or something—she is here organizing a wedding, isn't she?"

Luke snorted, his disbelief evident. "The guy was shirtless and cozied up next to her on the sand. No groom would be doing that two days before his wedding."

Fair point there, Reed thought, leaning back in his chair and studying his friend's downturned head as he tried to think of something else to say. Deciding a different tactic was in order, he tried, "Maybe you just caught her off guard, you know? She probably wasn't expecting to see you, and the two of you haven't spoken in five years, right? To hear those words out of the blue... they would probably stop anyone in their tracks."

He ran his fingers idly down his stubbled cheeks. "You could always try again," he suggested. "Someplace where you can be alone, just the two of you. Hash things out."

"Yeah, I don't think so." The dullness had returned to Luke's eyes as he shook his head slowly. "I think I'm going to hide out for the next couple days, wait for her to leave the island." He gave a soft laugh that belied his pained expression. "If there's one thing running into Lydia yesterday taught me, it's that I never, *ever* want to see that woman again." Then he nodded toward the television. "Watching the game? I heard the news they're planning to trade Piper to the Orioles. Can you believe that?"

Reed was caught off guard by the rapid shift in topic, but he recovered quickly and reached for the remote. "Piper was the best thing that happened to that team in the last five years. They keep that up, and I'm going to become a Yankees fan instead." As Luke snorted in agreement, he raised the volume on the television, then headed to the kitchen for two more beers and a bag of half-eaten chips—the best he could do on such short notice.

As he rummaged through the fridge, he caught sight of Luke on the couch, looking more relaxed than he had all evening as he watched the game. Right now, his friend needed a distraction, and Reed was more than happy to give it to him.

CHAPTER 12

"Mom, there's something I need to tell you."

Emery was fiddling with her cloth napkin, folding and refolding it before smoothing it out on her lap. Tana could see that her daughter's hands were trembling, and she was instantly on alert, her mind returning to the tearful phone conversation she'd seen through the window of Daphne's bakery the other day. Since then, she'd wanted to bring up the subject with Emery, but she hadn't known where to begin—her daughter was an adult now, and she didn't want her to know that Tana had been snooping on a private moment, however unintentional it may have been.

So it was with a casual voice that she said, "Sure, what's up," before taking a sip of her water and setting the glass back down on the table beside the bread basket and a small bowl of whipped butter, Tana's favorite. Mother and daughter had chosen to dine off-island that evening after enjoying a movie and some much-needed retail therapy, and Tana had to admit... she was in heaven. These opportunities had become fewer and farther between as Emery got older, and were practically nonexistent since she had moved to New York City.

Emery cleared her throat, rearranged her napkin once more, and then reached for a slice of bread and the butter knife, spreading it with hands that were still trembling slightly before setting it on her plate without taking a bite. "I don't even know how to say this," she murmured, glancing around the restaurant as if to make sure that no one else was listening.

The place was packed, and the next table was occupied by a group of women having a bachelorette celebration—between their high-pitched cackling and cheering in between the shots of liquor they were tossing back like water, Tana was having a hard time hearing herself think. No way would anyone overhear their conversation in this racket.

Emery hesitated again, then finally said something at the exact moment another celebratory cheer went up at the neighboring table; the bride-to-be got up and took a bow, her paper crown askew, then arranged the sash across her chest and sat back down, nearly tipping over her chair in the process.

"Sorry," Tana said to Emery, shaking her head and casting the group a look of blended annoyance and amusement. "I didn't hear a thing you said."

"That's okay." Emery fiddled with her water glass. "I didn't say what I wanted to anyway—I'm stalling." She exhaled softly and said, "I haven't been entirely honest with you about why I'm here, on the island. The truth is, I quit school. I had been falling behind on my classes, I lost my internship, everything was a disaster."

She was speaking faster now, as if once she started pouring out her heart, she didn't want to stop. Finally, Emery looked up and met her mother's gaze. "I was on academic probation, with every chance to turn things around. Instead, I just… walked out. And I'm still not sure why." She gave Tana a plaintive look. "I'm sorry, Mom. I don't want to disappoint you, which is why I've been avoiding the subject."

Tana's heart squeezed painfully as she met her daughter's eyes. She suspected Emery wasn't telling the whole truth, but she didn't have to—Tana knew with every part of her being what had happened. Emery had always been a top student, a go-getter, a girl who knew what she wanted out of life and had taken the necessary steps to make her dreams a reality. She had excelled in her first three years of college, so why now, when she was nearing the end, would things take such an abrupt turn?

There could only be one explanation.

A wave of fury and shame rose up within her— fury at Derek, once again, for tearing their family apart and irreparably harming their daughter; and shame at herself for not doing a better job of shielding Emery from her own marital drama. What must it have been like for her, on her own, reading about her parents' imploding marriage and her father's escapades on the tabloid websites, of all places?

Until now, Tana had naively let herself believe that Emery would steer clear of both the rumors and the ugly truths splashed across the press, but that had been nothing but wishful thinking on her part. After all, she couldn't even go to the grocery store without seeing Lucia's and Derek's faces slapped on the front cover of every checkout stand magazine, so why would Emery have been spared that same pain?

Tana was silent for a long moment after Emery's confession, fearful of opening her mouth in case she broke down completely... which was the last thing her daughter needed right now. Hands clenched tightly beneath the table, she squeezed her eyes shut for a few brief seconds to compose herself before she said, "I'm sorry, Emery. For everything."

Emery had been watching the table of women next to them, but at Tana's words, she tore her gaze from them and stared, horrified, at her mother. "*You're* sorry? You didn't do anything. This was no one's fault but my own—it wasn't even Dad's. It's not like I'm in third grade, dealing with my parents divorcing. I'm twenty-one years old, for crying out loud."

She cringed. "I lost it completely, and I can't even put into words how embarrassed I am for letting things get to this point. I'm afraid..." Her voice trailed off, and she suddenly became very interested in the bread basket. Tana waited patiently for her to continue, and when she did, her voice was ragged. "I'm afraid I've ruined my future. I gave up a once-in-a-lifetime opportunity, and now I'm just... lost."

"No." Tana shook her head vigorously. "No, no,

absolutely not—I won't have you thinking that way. Just look at me." She jabbed her thumb into her chest. "I'm in my mid-forties, starting over completely in a new town, with new friends, a new job, and you know what? I'll let you in on a little secret."

She leaned toward her daughter, her lips tipping up in a smile. "I'm absolutely *terrified*. But I'm also excited, because while the future brings with it so many unknowns, I believe that many of them will be wonderful unknowns." She rested her hand on Emery's and gave it a light squeeze. "You have your whole life ahead of you, and you're just getting started. I think…"

She hesitated, unsure whether to voice her opinion on the matter, but then decided to continue. "I think your decision to leave school goes beyond what happened between your father and me. Somewhere deep inside, you knew it wasn't right—and it took something like this happening for you to act on it."

For the first time, Emery's eyes held a glimmer of hope. "Maybe you're right," she said, "and Uncle Jax told me basically the same thing. It's possible I'm looking at this all wrong. I think I need to take some time to figure things out, decide on my next steps."

She gave Tana her first genuine smile of the evening. "Do you think Uncle Henry would mind too much if I stayed at the inn for a little while? Just until I can clear my head?"

Tana laughed. "I think Uncle Henry would never admit it in a million years, but he's glad to have you, me, and Jax as his houseguests. He's been by himself for far too long."

Emery fell silent for a moment, staring vacantly out the window at the darkening sky. Then she turned to Tana with a sly smile. "Speaking of Uncle Jax, what in the world is going on with him and Daphne? Whenever those two are in the same room, you could cut the tension with a knife." She held up the butter knife for emphasis.

Tana groaned and reached for it, then began heaping whipped butter onto a slice of warm, flaky bread. "Don't even get me started on those two, or else we'll be here all night."

THE NEXT MORNING, Tana woke up early, her heart in her throat, and slid on her slippers before padding down to the inn's kitchen. She brewed herself a strong cup of coffee, then added a dash of hazelnut creamer before wandering down the hallway toward the inn's front parlor. She stood in front of the picture window, her eyes on the early-morning coastline; a fog had settled low over the water, blurring out the sun just beginning to rise, but the seagulls were undeterred, circling low over the water to make their first catch of the day.

Today was an important day for the inn, and—somewhat selfishly—for Tana. The article in the *Maine Herald* was set to drop this morning, marking the official reopening of the Inn at Dolphin Bay. The inn's website had also launched last night… to crickets, of course, but Tana was hoping that would change after the newspaper began arriving on doorsteps and in email inboxes. Uncle Henry's inn was practically a Maine institution, and she firmly believed that their neighbors would spread the word that the beautiful old building was ready to welcome guests once more.

And she and Uncle Henry would be waiting for them with open arms.

As she stood at the window, Tana reflected on all that had happened over the past few months, at the unexpected twists and turns she'd encountered in life. She'd meant what she said to her daughter at dinner last night—that sometimes life threw curveballs when you least expected them. At the end of the day, how you managed to hit back at those curveballs was what truly mattered—and right now, Tana thought, straightening up and smiling as she saw Reed's golf cart putter into the parking lot, she knew with every fiber of her being that she had hit a home run.

She watched him as he slid out of the driver's seat, sunglasses flipped over his eyes, dark hair peppered with gray tousled, as if he hadn't bothered running a comb through it before he left the house that morning. Despite her protests that he didn't need to make the trip, Reed had insisted on catching the first ferry of the day to the mainland and scouring the nearby all-night supermarket for the first copy of today's *Herald*. As Tana took one last sip of coffee and set the mug on the windowsill, she saw Reed bending over the golf cart's passenger seat and emerging a moment later with a stack of newspapers.

"Hi," she greeted him breathlessly at the door seconds later, her eyes on the papers. "Did you read the article?"

"Of course not," he said, stepping inside and setting the newspapers down at their feet before pulling Tana into a long hug. He trailed his fingertips along her spine as he held her tight, and she could feel herself relaxing into him, some of her anxiety immediately melting away just by being in close proximity to him.

After a few moments, he released her, then bent down and slid the first newspaper off the stack. "You should do the honors."

Without further ado, Tana tore through the paper, letting the business and sports sections flutter to the ground as she finally located the travel section. There, on the front page, was a full-color picture of the inn's exterior, its fresh coat of paint shining under a cloudless sky, its wraparound porch dotted with beautiful new furniture, its battered old sign replaced with a brand-new one featuring the inn's updated logo, a dolphin splashing out of the waves, the island's stunning lighthouse in the background.

Tana quickly scanned her eyes down the article until she reached the end, then returned to the top of the page and read it again, more closely, her heart sinking with disappointment.

"This article is amazing," Reed murmured as he read it over her shoulder. "It hits on everything you talked about with the reporter—the inn's history, its importance in the community, Henry's dedication to it. Look, she even gave the new website a shout-out at the end. Tana"—he spun her around, his light blue eyes dancing with excitement—"before you know it, you and Henry are going to have more bookings than you can handle." He smiled softly and took her hand. "I'm so incredibly proud of you."

"Thank you." Tana swallowed hard, then realized with a rush of embarrassment that tears were pooling at the corners of her eyes. She turned quickly to wipe them away without Reed noticing, but he caught her hand, his smile quickly dropping as he saw her face.

"What's wrong?" he asked, removing the newspaper from her hands and setting it down. He cupped her face in his palms, forcing her to meet his steady gaze. With the pad of one thumb, he gently wiped a tear that was trailing a slow path down her cheek. "Were you not happy with the article?"

"No, it's not that." Tana sniffed and pulled away from him, searching the pockets of her robe for a tissue and dabbing her eyes. "I feel ridiculous for even thinking this, but..." She gestured toward the paper. "I was hoping the reporter would have put in there something about what I'd said, about how any women going through a hard time in their lives could still find solace and new beginnings."

She shook her head. "I thought maybe some good could come out of everything I've been through, that maybe I could help someone else. I also hoped—" She stopped short as she realized what she'd been about to say.

"What?" Reed prompted, reaching for her hand. "Tell me what's going through your head."

"It's silly, really, but I was sort of hoping…" She inhaled sharply, then let the breath out slowly as she cast her eyes out to the window. The fog was beginning to lift, revealing a brilliant sunrise that danced and rippled across the water as the day's first beachgoers set up colorful beach umbrellas and chairs on the sand.

Then she turned and met Reed's gaze, determined to let him know that her next words didn't diminish her feelings for him. "I was sort of hoping Derek would somehow see the article and know that despite what he's done to me, I'm okay. More than okay."

She gripped Reed's hand, holding on as if it were a life preserver in a raging sea. Which, in many ways, it was. "I love you," she said softly, standing on tiptoe to press a soft kiss to his lips. "You mean so much to me, and I can't put into words what it's done for me that you walked into my life when you did. I'm so lucky. I just…" She dabbed at her eyes again. "I think Jax was right. I think I need closure."

Reed cupped her face once more, his eyes searching hers. Then he smiled gently and said, "Then let's get you some."

CHAPTER 13

$\mathcal{L}$ ydia checked and rechecked her clipboard as she sat at a small table in the corner of her hotel's restaurant, nursing a cup of coffee and a plate of eggs—no pancakes for her; she would need all the energy she could get for the coming day. Out of the corner of her eye, she watched a young couple cozied up at the table across the room and felt a pang of jealousy when the man leaned over and tenderly tucked a strand of hair behind the woman's ear. They were both sporting wedding rings gleaming in the restaurant's overhead lights, and judging by that, along with their total obliviousness to the hustle and bustle around them, Lydia knew they were on their honeymoon.

And soon, Maura and Jared would be jetting off

to their tropical honeymoon as well—then this whole nightmare of a wedding would be nothing more than an unpleasant memory.

Lydia flipped a page on her clipboard and consulted her notes as she lifted her mug to her lips and took a long sip of coffee. Right now, according to the detailed schedule she'd mapped out with the couple, Maura and her bridesmaids were just beginning their hair and makeup, while Jared hit the island's golf course with his groomsmen. They would both spend the morning relaxing and getting ready for the main event, which would begin at two o'clock sharp.

But there was much to be done before then, and Lydia needed to be at the venue in thirty minutes if she wanted to get everything ready in time to give the bride a pep talk and see her down the aisle.

With that in mind, Lydia scooped up the rest of her eggs, took one last swig of coffee, and was just signaling for the check when she heard footsteps behind her. She glanced up in time to see someone sliding into the empty chair opposite her, and to her surprise—and horror—she saw that it was Maura.

And not the same glamorous Maura she'd encountered on a weekly basis for the past twelve months. Today, her bride-to-be was sans makeup, with pale skin and dark circles under her eyes, as if she hadn't slept a wink all night. She was wearing an oversized T-shirt and loose-fitting pants, and her normally sleek hair was tied back in a messy pony-tail. But none of that caught Lydia's attention as much as her eyes—they were red-rimmed and puffy, like she'd been crying for hours.

A feeling of foreboding settled over her as she recalled her conversation with Jared on the beach, followed by the awkward encounter she'd witnessed between the couple at their rehearsal. Had he gotten cold feet?

"Lydia, I'm sorry to intrude on your breakfast," Maura said, her voice raw. She cleared her throat and gestured to the small carafe of coffee sitting on the table. "May I?"

Lydia nodded, then glanced over to the empty table beside her. She stood, grabbed a clean coffee cup from one of its place settings, and handed it to Maura, who immediately poured a full cup and drained it in one long swallow. Then she reached into the pocket of her pants and pulled out a crumpled-up tissue, dabbing at her eyes and then her nose before toying with it in her hands, avoiding Lydia's gaze.

Finally, she sighed heavily and looked up, her

eyes dull and lifeless. "I guess I should just come right out and say it, although believe me, I know what I look like—I'm sure you can guess what's happened." She paused and pressed her fingers against her mouth, her eyes welling up with tears once more. "Jared and I... the wedding is off."

Before Lydia could open her mouth, Maura barreled on, "I'm sorry that you've put so much work into this and it's all for nothing. You'll still get paid, of course, and I'll make sure Daddy throws in a big bonus for all the ways you've gone above and beyond for me and Jared." She said his name quietly, her tone laced with regret. Then she fell silent again, staring at the mug, her hands wrapped so tightly around it that Lydia could see her knuckles straining.

"I'm so sorry, Maura." Lydia slid her clipboard off the table, then leaned forward and rested her hand on Maura's wrist. She couldn't imagine what the young woman was going through—ending a relationship was painful enough, but doing it in front of everyone you knew, on what was supposed to be the happiest day of your life?

Lydia felt a hot stab of anger at Jared for not extricating himself from the relationship sooner than this and saving Maura the excruciating embarrassment of having to tell everyone she loved that she was essentially being left at the altar. "Did he at least tell you in person?"

A hypocritical question, to be sure, which was why Lydia had asked it. The torment she felt over the cowardly act of walking out on Luke when he wasn't even home had haunted her ever since, and she didn't wish it on anyone else.

Maura blinked at her several times, then frowned. "He didn't tell me anything. I ended things." She set down her coffee mug. "Why would you assume Jared was the one to call off the wedding?"

"Oh, I…" Lydia's mind was working in overdrive as she quickly backpedaled. By now, Maura's puffy eyes were narrowed, and her attention was laser-focused on Lydia as she awaited an explanation. Deciding not to break Jared's trust by divulging their conversation on the beach two days ago, Lydia opted instead for a nonchalant shrug and said, "I thought I saw him looking a little distant at the rehearsal last night, that's all."

"Oh." Maura leaned back and toyed with the end of her ponytail. "Yeah, maybe you did—who knows. I'm sure he wasn't a hundred percent happy in the relationship either, but…" She picked up a spoon from the table and began fiddling with it absent-mindedly. "I knew things weren't right, you know? Ever since we got engaged… it's like I became another person, one hyper-focused on everything being perfect and getting all the details right."

She gave Lydia a tight smile. "Sorry about that, by the way. I think it was my way of trying to maintain control over the things I could, because I knew in my heart that something between me and Jared just wasn't right. He's a good guy, don't get me wrong, but…"

Her voice trailed off as she, too, spotted the honeymooning couple across the restaurant. Now they were holding hands across the table, oblivious to the two women watching them wistfully.

"Remember last week, at the coffee shop?" Maura said, turning her attention back to Lydia. "You asked me if I would still love Jared when he was old and gray and having a hard time getting out of bed. And I just… couldn't imagine being with him for that many years. It felt wrong, somehow. Ever since then, I've been going over your words, that image, again and again in my head. I think I said yes to Jared's proposal because I thought it was the right thing to do—meet a nice guy, date for a little while, get married, buy a house, have babies, the whole nine yards. But the more I think about those things, the more uncertain I become that I even want them in the first place. And at the end of the day, if I'm not fully committed to this marriage, I'm not being fair to Jared, and just as importantly, I'm not being fair to myself."

She gave Lydia a smile, genuine this time—happy, even. "I deserve to have a good life. We all do. And now is my chance to go out and grab it." She lifted her mug and drained the rest of the coffee, then flagged down the waiter, retrieving her credit card from her wallet and handing it to him as Lydia began to protest.

"This one's on me," she said, shaking her head. She reached forward and rested her hand lightly on Lydia's wrist. "Thank you again, for everything. You're an amazing wedding planner, one who goes above and beyond for your clients. If you ever need a recommendation, you know where to find me."

When the waiter returned Maura's credit card, she stood, then took Lydia's hands and pulled her into a hug. "Thank you," she whispered, her voice cracking.

Then she swiped at her eyes, which were filling with tears again. "Now if you'll excuse me, I'm going to go back to my hotel room and have a good cry.

Today, I'm going to mourn the loss of the future Jared and I planned together. But tomorrow…"

This time, she let the tears trickle down her cheeks without bothering to wipe them away. "Tomorrow is a new day."

She leaned in for one last hug, giving Lydia a brief squeeze as she whispered, "And I hope you find your happiness too, whatever it may be."

DAPHNE GLANCED up at the sound of the bell above the bakery door and saw Luke in the doorway, whistling as he looked around. "Wow, Daphne, I haven't seen it all set up like this yet—it looks amazing."

He stepped inside, shaking his head as he took in the full effect, then gestured to the display cases, sparkling-clean and waiting to be filled with treats for Daphne's first customers. "All you need to do is fill up those bad boys and you'll be sold out by the end of your first morning—and I'll place good money on that bet."

"Hard to believe that in a few short days I'll be able to officially call myself a business owner," Daphne said, stepping out from around the counter to greet Luke with a hug. She felt a zing of nervous energy run through her as they touched; she was dreading the conversation ahead, but she knew it was one they had to have. Both of them.

"Thanks for coming," she said, leading him to a table near the window and gesturing for him to take the chair opposite her. As he sat down and smiled at her, she got a good look at him for the first time—and saw the sadness etched in his smile, the detachment in his eyes. She hadn't asked him if he'd encountered Lydia, not wanting to pour salt in what was clearly still an open wound, but she saw now that she didn't need to—the answer was written all over his face.

Opening her mouth, she was preparing to launch into the speech she'd rehearsed when Luke began speaking first. "I'm sorry," he said, clenching his hands together on the table, "for leading you on."

He winced and raked his fingers through his hair. "I didn't mean to—believe me. I think you're an amazing woman, and the feelings I've been having for you are absolutely genuine. But Lydia coming back to town…"

He blew out a shaky breath. "I feel like I've been losing my mind, Daph. And it's become painfully aware to me that I'm not over her, which isn't fair to you. So I think it's best if we remain friends… if you want to, that is."

Daphne gave him a relieved smile. "I would love to. You're a great guy, and this"—she waved her arm in a semi-circle, indicating the bakery—"would never have happened without your guidance, your input, and your encouragement. And I mean that from the bottom of my heart. You've been instrumental in helping me change my life, and I'll never forget that. Besides," she added softly, gazing out the window toward the gently rolling ocean beyond, "we can't help who we're in love with, can we?"

When she looked back at him, she saw that he was studying her face closely. "Jax?" he asked. "I couldn't help but notice… something… whenever I was around the two of you."

Daphne waved a hand in the air. "Water under the bridge. But thank you, Luke, truly, for being honest with me. You're a good man, and you deserve all the happiness in the world." She hesitated, her eyes lingering on his. "Do you think…?" She left the rest of the question hovering in the air between them, but she saw a flash of pain in his eyes before he responded.

"No." His voice was firm but wistful as he stared

down at his hands. "Lydia and I aren't meant to be, I guess. Someday, hopefully, I'll be able to accept that."

"Well if you ever need someone to talk to," Daphne said, "you know where to find me. Okay?" She tapped him on the wrist, forcing him to meet her gaze.

He nodded. "Okay."

"Good." Daphne nodded, then slid out of her chair. "Now if you don't mind, I've been testing a new recipe for the bakery's grand opening, and I was hoping you could be my official taster. How do strawberry cream cheese muffins sound?"

Luke groaned and patted his stomach playfully. "I need to stop hanging around you so much. Reed's been bugging me to do more kayaking around the island with him, and now I know why. I'm starting to rock a spare tire."

Daphne laughed as she headed to the kitchen, returning moments later with a tray weighed down with freshly baked muffins. She'd worked her basic muffin recipe five different ways before finally landing on what she thought was the perfect blend of tangy and sweet, and she was eager for someone other than her to give them a try.

As she set the tray down in front of Luke, she noticed someone walk past the bakery out of the corner of her eye, but she didn't give it any thought until the bell above the door chimed and in walked Jax.

"Hi," he said, his eyes skating from Daphne to Luke and back again. "I'm sorry for dropping by unannounced—am I interrupting something?"

"Nope, nothing at all," Luke cut in. He stood, grabbed a muffin in each hand, and held them up to Daphne in a salute. "I have to get going anyway, but I'll text you my full review of the muffins in a little while. Spoiler alert," he added with a smile, "I think they're going to be a hit." Then he nodded to Jax and slipped past him, whistling as he pushed open the door and stepped out onto the sidewalk.

Jax watched the other man walk away, his expression inscrutable, but when he turned back to Daphne, she could see the familiar mischievous glint in his eye. "So you and Showalter, huh? Not a bad choice." He nodded toward the muffins. "May I?"

"Help yourself," Daphne said, deciding to ignore his comment about Luke. Who she was dating—or not dating—was on a need-to-know basis, and Jax definitely wasn't privy to her love life. Things were uncomfortable enough between them as it was; why add fuel to the fire? She wasn't sure either one of them could survive the explosion.

Jax thanked her and slid a muffin off the tray, peeling off the wrapper and taking a bite, careful to catch the crumbs in his hand. "This place is pristine," he said sheepishly when she raised her eyebrows at him in amusement. "I don't want to cause you any more work than you already have."

"Thanks," she said, shifting from foot to foot, unable to decide whether to join him at the table or keep her distance. She watched as he helped himself to a second muffin—apparently she was right about this recipe being a winner—before finally sitting down opposite him and asking, "Jax... why are you here?"

The words came out rougher than intended, and at the sight of him wincing, she shook her head and added, "I'm sorry, that's not how I meant it. I just meant... I thought we agreed to keep our distance, take baby steps, see if we can actually be friends. You, this..." She waved one hand toward him, then the muffins, and finished her sentence on a weary sigh. "Do you really think we're ready for this?"

"For muffins?" Jax asked playfully, and then, seeing her expression, he fell silent, toying with the wrapper for a few moments as the silence stretched between them, painful and filled with regret. Oh, what could have been, Daphne thought, her eyes on his profile as he turned to look out the window. She knew that first love was powerful, of course, but to still feel that way after so many years—after so many heartaches? Powerful indeed.

Jax cleared his throat awkwardly, the sound like a foghorn in the silence. "I need to ask for a favor. That's why I'm here."

"Oh… sure." There was no denying the flash of disappointment she felt, but Daphne quickly banished it. "What's going on?"

"Well, you remember I was telling you about the restaurant investor? The one who's opening up a new bistro in Miami Beach and wants to interview me for the head chef position?" Jax's voice had turned earnest, his eyes lighting up with the opportunity she knew meant so much to him. "He's planning a trip to Dolphin Bay specifically so he can sample my food."

"I do remember you mentioning that, yes." She more than remembered it; Jax's announcement had been playing at the corners of her mind ever since he'd made it. But she would never voice that aloud, especially to him.

"Great, well, he gave me a call the other night and told me he had to move up his visit—to this coming Monday." Jax shook his head. "Talk about last-minute, right? Anyway, I've been scrambling ever since to finalize my menu and gather all the ingredients, but there's something else I need… and believe me, Daphne, I would never want to put you out. I asked Tana and Reed, but they've got plans, and I even asked Uncle Henry." He snorted. "But with the cane and everything, well, I don't think he'll really be able to balance a tray and—"

"Jax." Daphne stopped him with a hand on his arm, and he gave a start, staring down at her hand and then back up at her. She withdrew it quickly, folding her hands on the table instead and cocking her head to ask, "Do you need a waitress? Is that what you're asking?"

"Yes. Please. I'll pay you, of course, and it'll just be for a couple of hours tomorrow night." He held his breath, waiting for her to respond.

In that moment, as they looked into each other's eyes, it hit Daphne for perhaps the first time that Jax might really, truly be leaving. She knew that he didn't plan to stay in Dolphin Bay forever, of course —he was only here to regroup and recover from the ordeal of losing his restaurant—but still… she thought they had time.

Time for what, she couldn't quite say. Just… time.

"Of course I'll do it," she said, ignoring the pit in

her stomach. "But you don't have to pay me—instead, I'll strike you a deal."

"Sure," Jax said, looking both surprised and pleased. "Whatever you want."

Daphne gestured toward the bakery cases behind them. "The day before I officially open for business, I have to move about a million pounds of cakes and cookies and pies and cupcakes into the shop. I could really use some help."

Jax grinned at her. "I'd be happy to. That's what friends are for, right?"

The smile Daphne graced him with in return was strained around the edges. "That's what friends are for."

CHAPTER 14

The silence in the house was so loud it was practically deafening. Luke wandered around from room to room, his direction aimless, often stopping to run his hand along a bookshelf or pick up some knickknack or other, examine it idly, and then return it to its spot without actually noticing he had taken it down in the first place. The house, he realized now, was much the same as it had been on the day she left—the pictures still hung on the walls, the curtains she'd picked out still billowed softly in the ocean breeze, her favorite oven mitt was still in the kitchen drawer.

It was a shrine. To her, to them, to what might have been.

To what *should* have been.

Not until he finally saw her face again did Luke realize that he had lived every day with the belief that they would one day work it out. That they would return to each other, safe in the knowledge that they were meant to be together. All would be forgiven—it already was.

He needed her. He loved her. He would give her the moon if he could, hang it above her pillow so it smiled down on her alone each night, illuminating the strands of starlight in her beautiful hair.

But she didn't want it. She didn't want him.

Luke found himself wandering into the bedroom they'd once shared, sitting on the comforter they'd selected together. He ran his fingers along the pillow she'd left behind, the side of the bed that had belonged to her then—that belonged to her still, though it was cold and empty now. He slid to the floor, his fingers grazing beneath the bed for the small box he'd left there, the ring that had always felt like part of his skin. He didn't need it anymore, but he couldn't sell it either.

He glanced out the window, toward the ocean, roiling today, its surf swelling and slamming against the rocks that dominated the coastline on the wilder edge of the island he had always preferred to call home. He watched the waves for a while, entranced by their ebb and flow, then his eyes sought out the horizon, the ferry a distant speck as it glided toward the mainland. Tomorrow morning, Lydia would be on that ferry. After that, he would never see her again.

It was time for him to accept that.

It was over.

Pocketing the ring, he glanced once more at the raging sea, decision made. Feet in his sandals, sweatshirt donned, he headed for the door, casting one final look at the wedding photo, still tucked away in the corner of the living room, their faces alight with happiness, the future theirs to grab and hold onto, as tight as they could before it slipped away like vapor, like a wave from the sand.

"Goodbye, Lydia," he whispered, then opened the door and stepped outside to begin building his future—a new one, a devastating one, but his all the same.

LYDIA HURRIED through the island's streets, as familiar to her as her own hand. The sidewalks were crowded on this beautiful weekend day, men and women strolling hand in hand, shopping bags dangling from their wrists, children licking melting ice cream cones that were dribbling over their fingers. For once, she didn't stop and gaze at them, mourning all that she had lost; for once, she was looking not at her past but at her future.

The streets became more winding, the scenery wilder as she hurried away from town, toward the more remote side of the island that she and Luke had once called home. She'd protested the move at first, wanting to be in the center of the action, wanting to be able to step outside her front door and breathe in the scent of hot dogs drifting up from the boardwalk. But once they entered the house, with its cozy rooms and windswept views from glittering floor-to-ceiling windows, she knew it was the place where they would grow old.

When she rounded a bend in the road, she caught sight of it—the sloped, gray-shingled roof, the cheerful blue paint, the small front porch with two side-by-side rocking chairs, the scene of many of their late-night talks and early-morning coffees. Her heart squeezed painfully as the memories overwhelmed her, but she approached the house anyway, climbing the whitewashed porch steps and knocking on the door.

Silence reigned, thick and prolonged. Her heart

sank as she glanced at the nearest window, open a crack to let in the refreshing breeze. She made a beeline for it, pressing her nose against the glass to try and see inside. The lights were off, the kitchen empty, the living room—what she could see of it—still and quiet.

Undeterred, she headed around the back, pushing aside the dune grass they'd always let grow wild around the exterior of their property, breathing in the fragrant island plants that bloomed around the yard. The door to Luke's shed was ajar, and her heart leapt as she strode toward it, rehearsing what she planned to say when she came face to face with him once more. But it, too, was dark, with nothing to greet her but the smell of cut grass and the faint odor of gasoline from the lawn mower that took up most of the small space.

She exited the shed and sank onto its wooden platform, composing herself as she looked around. In her mind—in all the daydreams she'd had as she tied up the loose ends of Maura and Jared's canceled wedding and helped tear down the venue décor—Luke had been home, waiting to greet her with open arms. This—this cold, empty, lifeless house—wasn't the plan.

Her eyes skirted the edge of the property as she

debated what to do, snagging on the worn dirt path that Luke had carved in the dense foliage by hand, with nothing but a handful of gardening tools and weeks of hard, sweaty labor. It led directly to the beach, their own private path to paradise, one they'd walked many times, both together and alone. Pushing her hair back from her face, she rose and headed for it now, knowing in her soul that she would find him there.

The walk took longer than she remembered, and though the day was warm, the wind had kicked up, blowing strands of hair into her mouth and swaying the leaves of the plants surrounding her. Her feet sank into the sand the moment they touched, and she kicked off her shoes, holding them in one hand as she picked her way around the seashells and sticks that had washed onto the beach, her eyes on the lone figure standing where the water lapped against the shore. He was holding something, his hand stretched behind his back, as if ready to throw whatever it was into the sea.

"Luke," she called, cupping her hands around her mouth. The wind carried her words away, so she tried again, louder this time. Only then did he turn around, but not before he launched his arm forward, his hand opening, a small object that glinted in the sun hurtling toward the waves before sinking beneath them forever.

If he was surprised to see her, he didn't show it; instead, his expression was strangely blank as he took one step toward her, then another, until they met in the middle of the sand, the wind still whirling around them, sand and sea spraying them in the face.

"I'm glad I found you," she said, her eyes locking onto his. "I've been looking for you."

He didn't respond, merely cocked his head slightly, their gaze never breaking.

Her nerves kicked up then, and part of her screamed at her to turn back, to catch the ferry to the mainland and return to the life that had become easy, routine, one foot in front of the other, just make it through each day.

But that wasn't what she wanted. She wanted the ugliness. She wanted the hard work, the tears, the apologies and the promises of a better future. She wanted him; all of him. For better or for worse, as they'd promised each other all those years ago.

"The other day, on the beach." Her words were nearly drowned out by the waves rushing to shore, the cries of the seagulls circling overhead. "I just wanted you to know… Luke, I'm still in love with you too. I'm sorry I didn't tell you sooner. I needed time, I needed to think, I—"

Before she could say anything more, he took a step forward, until their bodies were nearly touching. His gaze searched her face, and she could hear his soft exhale before he pulled her to him, eyes blazing, and their lips finally found home.

TANA HELD the fluttering paper tightly as the wind kicked up unexpectedly, nearly ripping it from her hand and cartwheeling it across the sand. She flattened it out as best she could on her knee, then retrieved her pen from the sand and brought the tip to her chin, tapping it absentmindedly as she considered what to write. What words could she say to someone who had broken her so completely, who had ripped her self-esteem to shreds and forced her to rebuild an entire new life from scratch? She wanted closure; *this* was closure. Her chance to pour out her soul on paper, to force him to understand the consequences of what he had done.

She had been sitting in the sand for an hour, and so far, the paper only bore two words: *Dear Derek.*

A shrill cry interrupted her thoughts, and she

snapped her head up in time to see a little girl and her father playing in the water, him holding her toes above the water and plunging them in every time the waves rolled to shore. A woman watched from farther up the beach, camera in hand, head thrown back with laughter. Nearby, an elderly couple strolled along the shore, hand in hand, while a group of young women basked in the sunlight, wearing sunglasses and floppy hats, gossip magazines in hand as they chatted amongst themselves. Tana idly wondered whether Derek and Lucia graced the pages of those magazines, and then, upon second thought, realized she didn't really care. That was a past life, a different life, one she couldn't get back— and wouldn't choose to if she could.

Inspiration struck her then, and she lowered the pen to the paper, writing four more words as neatly as she could while the edges of the paper lifted once more in the wind. When she was finished, she set the pen in the sand and read the words on the page over and over, a smile on her lips and tears in her eyes.

Thank you, and goodbye.

Then she stood, made her way to the water's edge, and tossed the paper into the swirling sea.

EPILOGUE

*F*or the first time in several months, Henry walked along the sand with just his own two feet. No cane, no sympathetic looks from passersby, no reminder that the days ticking forward were much scanter than the ones already left behind. His gait was slow but steady, with only the minor stumble here and there, and a surreptitious glance to make sure that no one was watching.

When he reached the water's edge, he looked over and saw a familiar figure standing to his left: Tana, her hands in her pockets, her eyes cast over the ocean. He debated stopping to say hello, but she looked... peaceful. Her face was turned up to the sky, her hair flowing around her shoulders, and her entire body looked lighter, as though a weight had been lifted off it. Not wanting to interrupt, he turned and walked in the opposite direction, looking for a quiet spot along the shoreline.

He found it a few minutes later, a pocket of sand free of beach chairs and umbrellas, coolers and colorful towels. Lowering himself to the sand with a groan, he arranged his legs in as comfortable a position as he could manage, then gazed out over the water. It was a brilliant blue today, a reflection of the cloudless sky, but summer would soon come to an end, bringing with it the gray waters and chilly days that called for mugs of hot cocoa and a roaring fire in the inn's parlor. He hadn't asked Tana yet whether any guests had booked a stay in the coming weeks; he didn't want anything to distract him from the task at hand.

He was about to have the most important conversation of his life.

With that in mind, he took a deep breath and began, his eyes still on the sea.

"Johnny, you don't know me, but my name's Henry Turner. And I'm in love with Edie." He shifted uncomfortably, propping himself up with his good arm. "Now I'm not usually in the habit of stealing another fella's girl, but Edie… she tells me it's okay. She doesn't know I'm here, by the way—I want to keep this conversation between you and me." He turned his eyes skyward, toward the puffy white clouds floating lazily over the water.

"I want you to know that I'll treat her right, the way she deserves to be treated. And I'm not trying to take your place—she loves you just as much as she did all those years ago. That hasn't changed, and I don't want it to. But as I'm sure you know, she's getting on in years—don't tell her I said that either— and so am I. No one knows how much time we have left, and you're testament to that. But Johnny, I want to spend whatever future I have with her by my side, and I think she feels the same way."

He took another deep breath, then let it out slowly, steeling himself for the last part. "So Johnny, I guess what I'm trying to say is… would it be okay with you if I married your wife?"

He stared out over the horizon for several long moments, watching a sailboat drift lazily on the waves, the sunlight dance patterns along the water, a lone dolphin leap into the air before disappearing beneath the surf. Then he smiled and said, "Thanks. Now don't let me keep you—I'm sure you have a lot going on, wherever you are. And so do I." He patted his pocket, feeling for the ring tucked safely inside. "I don't have a moment to waste."

Slowly, carefully, he pushed himself to his feet, steadying himself before inching his way back down the sand, his eyes on the town and, somewhere within it, the woman he loved. Like he told Johnny, he didn't know how much time he had left—but he did know one thing.

He wanted to spend it with her.

THANK you for reading **The Last Goodbye**, the fourth book in the Dolphin Bay series. The story continues in **The Vow**, available soon!

To be the first to know about new releases, sign up for my email list. I'll never share your information with anyone.

To stay connected, check out my Facebook page, send me an email at miakentromance@gmail.com, or visit my website at www.miakent.com. I love to hear from my readers!

And to help indie authors like me continue bringing you the stories you love, please consider leaving a review of this book on the retailer of your choice.

Thank you so much for your support!

Love,

Mia

~

MIA KENT IS the author of clean, contemporary women's fiction and small-town romance. She writes heartfelt stories about love, friendship, happily ever after, and the importance of staying true to yourself.

She's been married for over a decade to her high school sweetheart, and when she isn't working on her next book, she's chasing around a toddler, crawling after an infant, and hiding from an eighty-pound tornado of dog love. Frankly, it's a wonder she writes at all.

To learn more about Mia's books, to sign up for her email list, or to send her a message, visit her website at www.miakent.com.

Printed in Great Britain
by Amazon